Dan Bar Hava was born and raised in Jerusalem. Creativity was an essential part of his life early on, with music being the focus during teens and young adulthood, and writing thereafter. After serving in the military and phase one of higher education, Dan moved to the US. He has co-written the film *Falling Star* (aka *Goyband*), a romantic comedy featuring Adam Pascal and Natasha Lyonne; and *Brooklyn All American,* a coming-of-age sports tale. *The 36 Watchers* is Dan's first novel.

Dedicated to my lovely family for all their love and support, especially to Galia Ella and Tal, and to my dear friends Bree, Scott, Matti, Itai, Alisa, John, and Alex for their encouragement and assistance.

Dan Bar Hava

THE 36 WATCHERS

BOOK I: FALL

ל"ו

AUSTIN MACAULEY PUBLISHERS™

LONDON ∗ CAMBRIDGE ∗ NEW YORK ∗ SHARJAH

Ordering Information:
Quantity sales: special discounts are available on quantity purchases by corporations, associations, and others. For details, contact the publisher at the address below.

Publisher's Cataloguing-in-Publication data
Bar Hava, Dan
The 36 Watchers: Book I: Fall

ISBN 9781641829472 (Paperback)
ISBN 9781641829489 (Hardback)
ISBN 9781645366492 (ePub e-book)

Library of Congress Control Number: 2019937232

The main category of the book — Fiction / Thriller / Suspense

www.austinmacauley.com/us

First Published (2019)
Austin Macauley Publishers LLC
40 Wall Street, 28th Floor
New York, NY 10005
USA
mail-usa@austinmacauley.com
+1 (646) 5125767

Thanks to Michael for his friendship, mentorship, and support, and to Gary for a great editing experience.

It is said that at all times there are 36 special people in the world, and that were it not for them, all of them, if even one of them was missing, the world would come to an end.

Talmud, the central religious text of Rabbinic Judaism, as quoted by Wikipedia

You could not step twice into the same river. Time is a game played beautifully by children.

Heraclitus of Ephesus (c. 535 BC – 475 BC)

The beginning of knowledge is the discovery of something we do not understand.

Frank Herbert, Author of "Dune"

Prologue

Henry was walking his dogs back to his home when he saw the mail truck appearing in the distance, snaking its way up the long, winding path to his modest comfortable dwelling, hiding appropriately behind a few oak and pine trees.

In this part of the North Midwest, a measure of privacy was almost mandatory.

It was an interesting contradiction unto itself—if one didn't hide oneself, then folks assumed one had something to hide.

Rocky and Apollo, light and dark golden retrievers named after his favorite movie characters, were playing with each other in the morning mist.

He always felt that they were walking him, not he walking them; a welcoming thought that fit neatly into his new, retired self.

The air was crisp and clean with both remnants of summer warmth and hints of winter chill. Fall was a very short season here and Henry intended to enjoy every bit of it.

His wife and two sons were away for a few days. "Away from old war stories," as Sam, his younger son would put it. Henry didn't take offense. There was a healthy equilibrium in the Morgan family, between the imposing career of the father and the normalcy of the rest of the clan, especially now, that he was retired.

When he approached his doorstep, he noticed a package left by the mail truck.

He knew the mail truck driver was one of his undercover guards, so there was no alarm at the sight of a sizable manila envelope, a few inches thick.

Henry actually felt a small tinge of excitement. Although he enjoyed his newfound tranquility, part of him still longed for days gone by, when envelopes like this were routine.

When he picked it up, he noticed the sender's name and smiled. Steven was a comrade-at-arms, albeit from a very different department, dealing mostly with Middle-East affairs. Henry spent most of his personal and professional life in Europe, before and after the wall fell. He and Steven cut their teeth at Langley at the same time, all those years ago. They were good friends and their friendship didn't require constant reaffirmation. It was always there; solid, unwavering.

Steven retired a few years prior and unlike Henry, his retirement was very active.

As he promised, he dove right away into the world of books, TV, and movies based on his real-life experience as a special agent, with some measure of success.

Henry, after feeding the dogs, took the package to his study; something told him that he would need a drink so he poured himself a Hennessy and settled himself in his favorite warhorse of an armchair.

The package contained a small thin envelope and another manila envelope, stuffed with papers.

He opened the thin one first. It contained a letter.

Hey buddy,

How are things in the Midwest? Are you bored yet? Just kidding... I need your advice.

I came across this material and not sure what to do with it.

You will see that it was classified in the old way. Langley doesn't work like this anymore.

I do not know what to do with this, it could be the new Indiana Jones, it could be dangerous, it could be nothing.

I could give it to one of my writers and have it published as fiction, but I am not sure it's the right thing to do.

Please give it a read; you'll see why I sent you a snail mail with this material—I don't want any cyber footprint here until I make up my mind.

I would feel bad asking you this favor, but according to my calculations, you must be bored out of your mind right about now in this Midwest hell paradise of yours!

Later, S.

Henry smiled at the ending; he could hear his friend's voice throughout the written words. Old dog, new tricks was a phrase they kept throwing at each other, rightfully so.

A sip, a quick look around his comfortable study; relics of almost forgotten battles, a piece from the Berlin wall, a picture with Lech Walesa, and a few rounds of an AK-47.

A signed copy of Solzhenitsyn's Gulag, pictures of his family in the magnificent Black Sea region, not far from Crimea.

Steven was right; he WAS bored out of his mind. Curious, he opened the package.

Central Agency
Classification: Level 12
Verification class: Omega 9
Field report.
Subject: "Desert Rose"
Operative deep UC friendly Alpha X-12

The following report is part one of a result of a three-day debriefing of the subject, aided by members of the dramatic reconstruction unit to maximize impact. Operative wishes to convey that, although easy to dismiss as imaginative flights of fancy and/or results of highly sophisticated use of recreational hallucinogenic substances not yet known to the general public, the following depiction and reconstitution of information, timeline and events, real or otherwise by Desert Rose may contain information of interest and vital to national security.

It is the operative opinion that details such as the veil hierarchy and the ORMES/ MAG structure and function need to be examined with care.

There are numerous literary references in appendix A, at the end of part II, that may be of help regarding the aforementioned areas of interest.

In addition, the invisibility/dimension X/antigravity and 'so called' 'Mental-chemistry' effects depicted in the narrative should also be looked at dispassionately.

As to the fleeting references to the crown jewels, and to the ceremonial application of menstrual blood, both could most likely be dismissed without further consideration.

Needless to say, the highly innovative, imaginative, and controversial content of this report should be kept classified as it could stir high emotions at a time when calm and logical handling of recent global events is highly necessary and in short supply.

DUFAX-12

Chapter 1

"You're lucky that Chris wore me out," said Jenna into the tiny cell phone cradled on her shoulder, "You know I would've kicked your butt all over the court otherwise." Her best friend Stephanie took the bait. Smiling, Jenna stretched her legs over the ottoman and listened to a torrent of fake-injured pride, a signature of Stephanie's love for a good drama pouring from the receiver.

Jenna's body was in that happy state of exhaustion that makes one's limbs feel heavy and liquid. The silky night's light was dancing gracefully over the wall paintings and over a few pieces of furniture. Her cozy Park Avenue studio housed a chic collection of contemporary art and comfy, retro pieces, comfort food for the sense of home, like pancakes and maple syrup, apple pie with whipped cream or a Norman Rockwell painting.

Jenna liked soft pastel colors; they provided her with much-needed contrasting effect to the sharpness of her mind and her existence. Everything was clear to Jenna; including the need to lose herself in the welcoming warmth of a rust-colored rug, deep enough to sink her feet in.

Jenna also liked black-and-white drawings, an Escher reproduction, a Kandinsky print; they kept her company in this late, late happy hour.

Her promised treat, should she win the match—an old habit from her prep school days that persisted happily into adulthood—was an all-American PB&J sandwich. She munched on it lazily while listening to Stephanie.

Jenna was all about treats and rewards. It made perfect sense to her. It combined the two central elements of her rather straightforward view of the world in the best possible way, order and fun. You did what you were supposed to do—landed a new client, ran a half marathon, cleaned the bathroom—that was order. You get rewarded; now *that* was fun. The size and scope of the rewards didn't matter. It could be a new book, an extra cup of coffee (awesome!), or a trip to Alaska. It was the feeling that counted.

The creamy peanut butter mixing with the sweet tang of jam and the solidity of the freshly baked bread—divine! And thank you, New York City, for small miracles. It was a couple of years ago when a sudden migraine sent her into the night and to the local pharmacy. There, hiding in the back of the nondescript CVS, she discovered the beauty of a 2 am shipment of freshly baked breads, bagels, and donuts. She was asked by patrons and workers alike to not advertise this to the world and has been enjoying it sparingly; the city that never sleeps can afford to not diet, occasionally.

"You're absolutely right," Jenna said with mock humility as the stream from the other side started to subside. "Rematch tomorrow?" asked Stephanie.

Usually, Jenna wasn't in the mood for so much squash in one week, but hey, it would be good for the less-than-perfect waistline that she was starting to notice in the mirror. Worse—Chris was starting to notice it too, although he was too polite to say anything.

One PB&J equals two squash matches—good math!

"You got it, Steph," she said. "I'm going to turn in as well, just a quick email check and an early wake-up call. Tom wants to see the presentation before the clients get in from wherever-the-hell they are coming from…" Like most of her friends and co-workers, Jenna had a tendency to divide the world into New York (and by New York, she really meant the New York map in the back of a yellow cab—South St. seaport to the north end of Central Park on 110th street) and everywhere else.

The slender Mac was on the nightstand and Jenna was multitasking while waiting for the email to pop up. As she deleted spam, she noticed an email from her uncle, Josh, which was extremely unusual. Uncle Josh was an anomaly in her twenty-first-century existence, a staunch relic from a bygone era. He lived in Jerusalem for most of her life but never applied for Israeli citizenship. His numerous books on history, philosophy, and religion were a constant in an otherwise constantly shifting books landscape in her several New York City apartments, although she was never able to finish reading any of them.

Their somewhat anachronistic pacing seemed like intellectual slow-mo to her bottom-line driven, New York minute mind. She did pick up some intriguing conversation pieces from those books however: facts like where the world's oldest mummy came from (China and NOT Egypt), and the various theories about the brothers and sisters of Jesus, electricity in ancient Baghdad, the origin of the Friday the 13th superstition, definitely party favorites in the right parties.

Josh was short and stocky. Jenna and most of her family were thin and long-limbed, which perhaps came from her father's side. Jenna could recall old photos of slim, long-limbed ancestors in her father's study. If color photography had been available those days, you could have seen the reddish hair, a somewhat unusual genetic trend in an East-European Jewish dynasty. Perhaps the red hair was a remnant of some less-than-holy encounter with Viking raiders or Cossack riders down on the misty wharf of some long-forgotten river.

Jenna was thankful for her genetic package. "Eye candy with brains," her uncle used to call her during and after her college years. Indeed, the upturned nose and bluish-green eyes hailing from under a canopy of soft, red curls hid a sharp and cunning mind with more than a gesture towards irony. And the best part was that they were completely unexpected qualities given her oh-so-cute appearance.

One may think that Jenna would constantly have to fight a less-than-serious attitude towards her from the world, particularly from the MEN of the world.

This was usually not the case—most people did notice the steel-like logic and composure that lay underneath the cute-as-a-button appearance.

Jenna rarely had to assert herself, but when she did, you better take five steps back; she meant business. She was now curious about the email; it was sent minutes ago. What could her uncle want?

Despite his unremarkable features, Uncle Josh was extremely intriguing. Quite a few times, he helped Jenna with work and gave phenomenal advice on apartments, boyfriends, and the stock market. He was a lifelong bachelor and since

Jenna's parents moved to Israel a few years prior, Josh was increasingly there for her, filling the void she was quick to deny existed whenever asked.

Her parents were die-hard Zionists and supporters of the Jewish state. They refused to hear anything that would criticize Israel even a little bit. Jenna shared their love of this faraway land but with a healthy dose of an outside perspective. This made for many dinner discussions becoming loud arguments when topics like the Israeli-Palestinian fight, the Israeli-Arab conflict or who has rights to Jerusalem's holy sites were brought up.

Although there was plenty of love between Stanley and Amy Berg and their only daughter, it wasn't necessarily a bad thing to put some five thousand miles between parents and offspring.

Uncle Josh stepped quite naturally into a parent-like role, and Jenna wasn't sure what she was enjoying more—the closer relationship with her quirky uncle or the comfortable 'long-distance thing' with her parents. "Well, at least they didn't move into an actual settlement!" she used to say. Stanley and Amy were considering becoming hardcore West Bank settlers in that hotly contested territory, sharing a hillside with a few dozen zealots and a few hundred, less-than-friendly Palestinian Arabs.

But security concerns prevailed and they settled in a cozy villa in Kfar Shmaryahu, an affluent suburb just north of Tel Aviv and a mere twelve miles from the West Bank. After all, it was Israel. Everything is a stone's throw away from everything else, with many stones being thrown to attest to that assertion.

"Dear J," said the computer in a steady news-anchor-type voice as Jenna was cleaning her contact lenses. Josh's email was weirdly formal, as he wasn't used to email communication. He wrote as if it was an old-fashioned, snail mail letter. That particular quirk always made Jenna smile.

"I hope everything is well with you and yours. I know you are wondering why I didn't call you." "Yeah, why?" Jenna's mind was absently musing, focusing on the task at hand. Too many times, she would spend precious sleeping minutes hunched on the floor looking for a contact lens that jumped from her hand and hit the rug noiselessly, disappearing from view on the gleaming bathroom tiles and leading to a long, frustrating search.

"…well this is extremely important and I am actually afraid that someone may be listening to my line." *That* was a bit unusual. Uncle Josh has had his paranoid spells, but not in a while. Jenna had forgotten how he could sometimes become a trifle strange. "Must be all these years in Jerusalem," she used to think. "All those crazies around you, you are bound to pick up some of the craziness yourself."

"Well, Darling Niece, I am asking you to do something for me," continued the voice. Jenna could have stopped the voice feature as she was ready for bed, but she was comfy, lazily stretched diagonally on the copper-colored sheets. In a strange way, the computer voice was a substitute for the presence of her uncle, with his 'wells' and 'indeeds', his archaic way of communicating and his somewhat unusual speech patterns.

"I need you to call in sick tomorrow," said the computer. Jenna was somewhat startled, but not too much. Uncle Josh's requests were few and far between and usually rather weird, just like this one.

"You might consider this request a very strange one indeed," continued the computerized uncle. "I can't get into the reasoning right now, as it is a bit complicated." "I bet it is," she was thinking. Josh and his understated manner of expression often found Jenna treading the line between amusement and annoyance. She had to admit though that he was always right, an annoyance in and of itself.

"...but it is of the utmost importance that you stay home tomorrow. Please trust me, Little One." Little One was his nickname for her when she was in braces over a decade ago. Jenna's mind, concentrated on her uncle's intrusion into her habitual routine, only took slight offence at hearing this long-forgotten nickname. "I know your presentation is due tomorrow," Uncle Josh continued, "but I am sure Tom will understand. After all, you are an outstanding, brilliant, and creative junior copywriter, AND my niece."

"How the hell does he remember everything?" Jenna was wondering. She would put up a fight, but Josh's impressive performance of total knowledge of her life yet again crippled her defenses.

"I know you will do the right thing, Little One," said the screen. "I will contact you sometime tomorrow and explain, *laila tov.*" "And good night to you too," thought Jenna, somewhat angry at her uncle's power to make her yield to his will. He had to end his email in Hebrew, reminding her that he knows more, A LOT more than she does. Jenna knew that she would comply. Josh had helped her a lot and was quite generous at gift-giving, as various pieces of jewelry, one or two cars, and great trips could attest to.

She dialed Tom's voicemail. "Hey Boss, it's Jenna. I am so sorry to spring this on you last minute, but I can't be there tomorrow, a family emergency. I will call in later and check with Kenneth. I am sure that he will be able to handle the clients for one day. Thanks, boss!"

Jenna could afford this. Her last day off was over nine months ago. She was pushing for a promotion and her record was exemplary. Of course, now she would have to push a bit harder, as management did not look too kindly on last-minute sick calls. Jenna's reputation would take a bit of a hit, but she would recover.

After all, she was the one that always found the right way to persuade the client, she was the one that remembered the final marketing lesson from her professor.

The lesson about the choices, the lesson that taught her that there was always one more choice to land that account, to get the client to go with her vision, to get that new job, to score that big promotion. If the first choice doesn't work and the second crashes and burns, there is ALWAYS a third way; this was branded into her mind and had helped her more times than she could count.

She was the one who figured out a way to reach multiple demographics with a whole bunch of products that no one actually needed, wanted, or would ever use. That is the 'essence of marketing' as the higher-ups used to say. Make them buy it, like it, and forget that they actually don't really need it; whatever IT was.

"I hope you are worth it, Uncle," she was thinking, as her mind was drifting away. Just as she fell softly into a peaceful sleep, the clock on the nightstand turned.

The bright red letters and numbers announced, "12:00 AM Tuesday, 9/11/2001."

You're nothing but a pack of cards!
Alice in Wonderland, Lewis Carroll, 1865

Chapter 2

It was a seemingly odd scene, thought Stephanie as she was sipping her coffee—or what was accepted as coffee here. At least, it was hot and had some remnant of taste; she had had worse. But then again, when you are spoiled for a few months by real coffee made by a real Italian, you are pretty much screwed. Choice beans, choice pot, just the right amount of milk, just the right amount of heat.

At times, it seemed that Stephanie kept that particular boyfriend around for as long as she had because of his coffee-making abilities, not to mention the made-from-scratch Marinara sauce and authentic Milan-style ravioli. There were other reasons, but "in sum, what impressed you, my sweet selfish bastion of happy womanhood, is the K-room, not the B-room; after all, that, which lingers longer is more impressive."

She caught herself, somewhat surprised that she could immerse herself in such an irrelevant subject today of all days. Perhaps it was the feeling of unexpected…was it tranquility? Was it a healthy dose of escapism? Or was it just aftershock? Stephanie wasn't sure. Her positive, happy, sassy mind was straining against the day's events.

She was sitting in the small and cramped lounge area of the Mount Sinai Hospital ICU. She expected things here to be more: more noise, more intensity, more panic, and more people. Stephanie worked for the Manhattan district attorney and had been in her share of hospital waiting rooms. She fully expected the mayhem outside to invade the inside as well.

But on this day, this fateful day, her city turned upside down. It seemed that here there was almost an island of calm and professionalism that helped her regain some calm as well. She could feel her overstretched and numbed mind actually regaining some strength and comfort from the display of quiet efficiency around her, an answer to the forces of evil that dealt a deadly blow to her beloved city.

Stephanie was a combination of contrasts, a 'walking contradiction', as Jenna loved to call her before, during, or after one of their many fake arguments, and/or mock fights about relationships, body fat and lifestyle, politics, religion, neighborhoods, career choices, coffee—you name it. Another sip, *I can almost hear Jenna say,* "Barely diner-acceptable," she thought, trying, with only partial success, to contain her anxiety.

Jenna, with her tendency to answer a question with a question and love of long, endless arguments, was Jewish, but in the words of the immortal Mel Brooks, "Not too Jewish." Stephanie, with her affinity for drama and extra sass, was Latina, but not too Latina. For both friends, there was really one color—New York. Everything else was so last century, and Jenna's newish acquisition in the New York meat market, Chris, fit perfectly into that happy landscape.

All three shared the same color-blind vision, and all three shared a happy, politically incorrect sense of humor. "Equal opportunity offenders," Jenna, who knew the best Jewish jokes, used to say.

Jenna was the uptown girl, Stephanie, the downtown girl. Jenna would poke holes in everything, and Stephanie would try to mend them—cynical versus caring, not that Jenna wasn't caring, and not that Stephanie didn't know how to unleash wit and cynicism if the scenario required it.

Their respective dispositions were of one woman who was out to get the world, and the other one who would protect it.

Jenna was the girl with the 'to-do' lists. Stephanie would forget to show up. Stephanie was probably the only human at whom Jenna wouldn't get mad for fifteen to twenty minutes of tardiness. "I just lost track of time in the garden with some of the neighborhood kids," she would say with a seraphic smile that always seemed to melt away Jenna's half-real, half-fake anger and at most times, would avoid a sly comment on Latina time.

Stephanie was short, and had unruly and intense dark hair. She was not traditionally pretty and definitely carried a few extra pounds. It was no small wonder that men found Stephanie attractive and compelling as often as they did.

Stephanie was a considerable nemesis and a large source of frustration to the herds of yoga mat-carrying, calorie-counting, gym-obsessed, processed, and carefully manicured females that swarmed about—annoying to all except Jenna. "Laurel and Hardy," they used to be called in their NYU days. Slim Jenna and stocky Stephanie, an inseparable couple.

Perhaps it was the energy. Stephanie had a bright disposition—an exciting aura about her. Everything she did was done with power, with gusto, and with sheer enjoyment. She didn't pretend not to care about how and what she said or did. She actually DIDN'T care. "Geek is the new cool," Stephanie used to say, "and I am queen of the geeks." Maybe it was that quality that made it possible for her to avoid scrambling for a date on a Friday night, or Saturday night, or any other night for that matter.

So they argued—Jenna was trying to get Stephanie out of junk food and into having an organizer. Stephanie would try to get Jenna to see more magic and less irony. To not always look for the last word, and to go with the flow.

"Sometimes, I wish I could shrink your brain just a little bit," Stephanie used to say after Jenna named all 50 states in less than five minutes or slew another sacred cow in a never-ending battle. "You don't have to be so Jewish all the time!" Which, of course, led Jenna to flare up some more and eventually to both friends collapsing in a fit of laughter, until the next time.

Jenna would constantly try to take Stephanie out of her beloved East Village hangouts and into her Park Avenue habitat. Stephanie would constantly try to get Jenna to spend more time below 14th Street…but not now, not today. Stephanie was half smiling, absently remembering, "Now I would be happy to go to the Upper East Side for you, girl…"

Stephanie was thinking, "Now I am waiting for permission to go in and see my friend. My friend that I thought I lost, Jenna, dearest Jenna. I don't know by what miracle you survived today, but I am not questioning. I am just happy to be here, if I can use this word on this day. I am though, I really am. I really thought I'd lost you."

In a strange way, it was good for her to be here, on that terrible day, in a hospital waiting room. The memories are so vivid, so etched into her consciousness—feeling the unexplained and unexpected THUDD, walking outside and being told by the super that, "A plane hit the World Trade Center." "A WHAT hit the WHAT?" was her reaction. Unthinkable, incomprehensible, unreal…

But there it was. As soon as she reached Houston Street, she saw that sickening sight. She instantly knew that this sight would stay with her, deeply etched in her brain for a long, long time— thick, black, vile clouds of smoke rising from the towers, as unreal as it seemed, like the B-rated disaster films that she never cared for—WW III, the day after, nuclear holocaust. Alien invasion…

As much as her mind refused to grasp what was happening in front of her unbelieving eyes, she knew that this devastating sight would never go away, would always stay vivid in her mind's eye.

It was as if, for a sliver of a second, her mind went through a freeze-frame process. It was a very quick freeze frame: clouds, light clouds in the blue sky, deep smoke rising, no sound track, and just sickening sight. Sickening silence.

And then—then it was all a blur—scrambling uptown, phones down, watching in horror as the towers fell, as people were jumping, finding a landline to call her parents, friends. And in the middle of all this, it hit her—Jenna!

Stephanie actually forgot that Jenna's firm relocated to the twin towers just weeks ago. It simply slipped her mind in the turmoil of that fateful day.

When she put two and two together, it suddenly hit her…

Physically nauseating shock, disbelief, pain, fear, and anger… Stephanie didn't know what to do or what to think—911 crashed under the load. Her own office had been evacuated. "Should I go down there? Where are the survivors? DID Jenna survive? Was she—God? No, no, no!" And then, the call came, only moments later. She couldn't believe it. She couldn't believe that voice on the other end, telling her that her best friend was still alive, telling her that in the evening she could come and visit.

And now, she was here. Doctors had been cryptic when she asked them why she couldn't go in yet. But then again, doctors are always cryptic. "So sip this bad coffee, Stephanie, and wait patiently. This day, this terrible day, would just get better from now on. It pretty much would have to now, wouldn't it?" she said to herself.

A familiar voice invaded her reverie.

"I can't believe you're drinking hospital coffee." She recoiled, raising her eyes. "Chris, you made it!"

He nodded and smiled. Stephanie got out of her seat and gave him a warm hug.

"How the hell did you make it across the Brooklyn Bridge?" asked Stephanie.

"I thought they locked us in pretty tight after the little trouble we had downtown this morning," she said and smiled at him. As always, Stephanie was determined to eclipse Chris in his understated way of stating things, even today, especially today.

"We did have a bit of trouble," he said and nodded his approval. "And they did seal us in pretty tight," he said, smiling back at her. "But I still have some friends," he said, with his disarming smile, the one that made her think about Denzel Washington in—what was that movie?

"…and don't start that again. I get plenty of that from Jenna," he said, referring to the frequent questions about his past that never ceased to amuse Stephanie and Jenna, who supposedly asked in order to annoy Chris. Amusement and annoyance had a pretty thin line separating them.

His smile was returned generously, accompanied by a warm hug, and deriving assurances from the touch of friendly flesh. Letting go of the understatement, they both felt comfort. Comfort was in short supply today and they appreciated each other in a way that only true friends do. Under the pressure of the day's events, people can hurt each other or grow strong with each other. They grew strong. They had to—for Jenna.

They sat, temporary happiness seeping in, replacing some of the shock and disbelief of the day.

Chris was one of those rare beings that Stephanie and Jenna prized, from day one.

They were seated at a downtown bar when the waiter brought a drink and a note that said:

"To the brunette girl:

1. Can you please tell your friend that I can't stop looking at her, and
2. Please tell her that I have never EVER done this before—sending a note to a strange girl at a bar, and it is such a fucking cliché, but I just didn't know what else to do."

It was the mixture of sincerity, profanity, and originality that both girls found amusing, and in Jenna's case, irresistible.

They could never agree on whether Chris was telling the truth when he sent that note. Somehow, it walked the line between disarmingly spontaneous and smoothly calculated. "One could almost hear Sade's 'Smooth Operator' playing in the background as if this was a movie scene," Stephanie said once when discussing this, getting slightly under her friend's skin in true Stephanie fashion.

They agreed that he must have been more than just 'ex-military', which is how he liked to describe himself. They agreed that he was good for Jenna; and most of all, they agreed that he should get the hell out of that Brooklyn dwelling of his and move into the real city.

For his part, Chris enjoyed defending the rough-and-tumble Prospect Heights neighborhood, stating correctly that it was the only place one could get a thousand-plus square foot loft/house WITH an outdoor space without mortgaging his family's entire future. "And one of the few places in the city where a black man can enter his front door without the cops thinking he may be robbing the place," he used to joke, or half joke.

He was working in private security and would occasionally take Jenna for rides in his Road King. She reluctantly agreed, and was resistant at first but learned to enjoy the experience.

He was in his early thirties, tall but not too tall, slim but not too slim and handsome, but not too handsome. He was a good combination of seriousness and fun, and often found himself in the middle of one of the never-ending debates between the two friends. Chris and Jenna were at the stage of dating that hovered on the threshold of entering the next level of seriousness, but both of them were taking their time, enjoying the lightness, and playing it day-by-day and weekend-by-weekend.

They knew that even in this day and age, twenty-first century and all, eyebrows would still rise. An interracial couple was—thank god—not that rare anymore, but still they would have to face some issues if/when they moved to the next level, so the in-between worked well for both.

They were set in their ways; Jenna in her organized, regimented, and exciting world, and Chris in his non-9-5, non-routine-routine and the go-with-the-flow flair.

Stephanie was happy he was there for herself as much as for her friend.

"Coming here did pose a bit of a challenge," said Chris in his understated way and Stephanie knew it must have been VERY hard.

"Did you ride here?" she asked.

"I wish," he said and smiled the slow smile that both girls enjoyed so much.

"For a while, they actually closed down the bridge and subway service stopped, but I made it. Steph, how is she?"

"Doctors won't say," said Stephanie. She decided that she liked it when he called her Steph. He claimed that it reminded him of one of his army buddies and she didn't mind.

"They didn't tell you anything? Why she is here? Is she seriously hurt?"

Now more than ever, Stephanie appreciated his calm and collected manner and his matter-of-fact way of communicating.

"Nope, they just told me to sit tight." "Doctors will be doctors," he said. Stephanie smiled; those were HER words.

"I guess it is just us," he said, "What with her parents being in Israel and all."

"Yup, it will take them a long time to get here. Besides, I don't think the hospital notified them yet. International lines are still down."

"So Jenna listed both of us as emergency contacts? I'm honored!" he smiled. "You should be," she said, "You guys haven't been dating THAT long."

"Excuse me—are you here for Miss Berg?" a robed doctor asked as he approached them, chart in hand. He was tall, slim, with lightly receding hairline and an aura that inspired trust, like the doctors you'd see on TV, like the doctors you would WANT to see in real life when you needed them.

Both rose to their feet, responding to the aura of professionalism and sincerity. "Yes," said Stephanie, "Can you please tell us what's going on? Can we go see her?"

"Hello, I am Doctor Martin, brain trauma department."

Chris looked stunned. Stephanie was first to respond even though she was shocked as well. Brain trauma was the last thing they expected to hear.

"B-brain trauma?" she asked in a small voice. "What is wrong with Jenna?" The doctor's experienced eyes flickered on both of them.

"You haven't been told, haven't you?"

"Told what?" asked Chris, exchanging looks of grave concern with Stephanie.

Dr. Martin didn't mince words.

"Jenna is in a coma," he said, eyes on them, better to get it out at once. They were both speechless; the doctor gave them a bit of time to adjust.

Just as he was going to move things along, Stephanie, once more the quicker one, responded.

"Coma?" whispered Stephanie. "I've been told she wasn't at the towers." "She wasn't." Agreed Doctor Martin. "It's something else."

"Like what?" asked Chris, seemingly calm but with an undercurrent of urgency and concern. This wasn't his first rodeo, tending to friends and loved ones in hospital beds.

"Just a moment please," said the doctor, checking something on his chart. "I take it none of you are family."

"That's right," said Stephanie. "Jenna's parents live in Israel and she is their only daughter. There is also an uncle, but he travels frequently and is probably out of town. I am her best friend and Chris is her boyfriend."

The Doctor looked at them and managed a quick smile.

"I apologize for keeping you in the dark." His hand described a half arc.

"Usually, we only discuss this with kin. But today—I guess today is unusual for many reasons, so you will have to do." He smiled to take away the edge of his words.

Their worried eyes were on him.

"Coma?" whispered Stephanie. "What the…?"

"Yeah," said Chris. "If she wasn't hurt by the terror attack, then why is she in a coma?"

Stephanie threw a quick appreciative look at him, "He sure is rolling with the punches," was her thought.

Doctor Martin looked a bit less confident.

"We are not really sure," he said. "I was hoping maybe you could shed a little light on the situation."

"Us?" asked Stephanie. "Why us?"

"Well, all I have here is a statement from the EMS people. They said that the super of her apartment building was responding to calls of neighbors that complained about excessive noise from Jenna's apartment. One of the neighbors said that he heard screams and things being thrown around. When the super finally opened the door, he found Jenna unconscious."

His eyes studied them again.

"You wouldn't know anything about that now, would you?"

They both shook their heads silently, absorbing the shocking revelation.

"Do you know of anything that could have done this to her?" asked Dr. Martin. "Any stress she was under? Work? Money? Anything?"

They both shook their heads. "Relationship issues?" That was addressed to Chris, and before he could answer, Doctor Martin dismissed the question. Chris's concern and demeanor were answer enough for THAT particular question; no relationship issues. "Pity," Dr. Martin was thinking to himself, "I wish it were THAT simple."

He was looking at them; they were taking it as well as could be expected. He sighed.

"Well," he said, "that is the story then. That is how we got her; she simply hasn't woken up since EMS picked her up. All her vitals are steady and there is no visible sign of any serious physical trauma. It's as if she is sleeping, but she is not. She is in a coma and it is a deep one."

"How deep?" asked Chris. Dr. Martin shot a quick look at him. Chris smiled faintly. "Yeah, I do know a bit about this," he said, his smile aimed at Stephanie who looked at him wide eyed.

"Is her score low? Do you consider her a level one?"

Dr. Martin looked at him thoughtfully and nodded, "Affirmative for both," he said.

"What on earth are you guys talking about?" exclaimed Stephanie.

"I'm sure your friend can explain this to you," said the doctor. He was obviously getting ready to wrap this up. "Her vitals are strong and that is a good sign."

They took a moment to digest the mixed message in his voice, the silver lining that was displaying on the monitors in her room versus the unknown reason that plunged her into this deep, unexplained state.

"Can we see her?" asked Stephanie, petrified but determined not to show it. "Oh yes," said Doctor Martin, "In fact, you can help."

"By talking to her?" asked Chris.

Doctor Martin eyed him and said, "You know," not a question, a statement. Chris nodded thoughtfully.

Stephanie looked at them both. "You guys care to fill me in on all this levels, scores, and talk stuff?"

"There is not a lot we know about these deep coma situations," said Doctor Martin. "But there is some evidence that friendly voices may have a positive impact on the recovery process."

He paused, their eyes on him; time for a bit more reinforcement.

"In fact, I am fairly convinced that friendly voices can make all the difference," he said. Less than scientific, but some moments call for a less-than-scientific approach.

"So you want us to sit in...in there and talk to her?" asked Stephanie.

"Oh yes," agreed the Doctor. "Tell her stories, tell her about your day, tell her about what you watched on TV. Tell her about dinner, anything you want, anything is better than silence."

His tired eyes rested on them. "So—can I count on you?"

He already knew the answer.

"Now, if you will excuse me, I have a major terror attack to attend too." His eyes defied his words and both Stephanie and Chris smiled along with him. Dr. Martin was definitely an improvement on the usual condescending fare that they were both accustomed to when it came to doctors, hospitals, and health professionals in general. One of Stephanie's favorite jokes would attest to this notion:

"What is the difference between God and a doctor? God doesn't think he is a doctor…"

As it ran through her mind, it made her flash her special smile, that disarming, carefully blended combination of "I know better than you" and "Please, oh please teach me the ways of the world."

Both men absorbed and recoiled. Stephanie was idly amused that, no matter what, men will always be that—men, a comforting thought on this very non-comforting day.

"Frankly, your Jenna was a welcome diversion from today's horrors," said Doctor Martin. He was having a hard time hurrying to return to the reality of the day. He was savoring those last few seconds with these nice people before plunging back into the pool of misery that was that day, his day.

"Now go and keep her company you two. I will be watching."

They were watching him leave and Stephanie turned to Chris.

"What was all that about?" she asked him. "Are you a doctor as well as security?"

"Not quite."

"So?"

"In my line of work, you learn about these things. Coma is measured primarily by three different indicators, eye movements, verbal responses, and motor responses."

"The greater response the higher the score. That's why I asked him about the low score."

"And Jenna has a low score," she whispered, understanding slipping in. "Yes," he agreed, doing his best to mask the deep worry he was feeling.

"Low score means no response."

"But you guys talked about something else—levels, something about levels."

Chris nodded; "That's a different way to look at it. There are two ways to look at coma. I was curious that the doctor was considering both ways. I do like the first one; it is simple. They call it the Glasgow method."

"The Glasgow method? As in Scotland?"

"I guess so," he said, "And don't ask me why. I am not THAT knowledgeable."

She punched him playfully, appreciating his attempt at making light of the situation. "I don't make any promises," she said tit-for-tat.

What doesn't kill us makes us stronger.

Friedrich Nietzsche

Chapter 3

"So, I took advantage of the fact that you're here and took your parents to a restaurant downtown," smiled Stephanie. "I think they were so petrified by my neighborhood that they actually forgot to worry about you for the duration of dinner. They even let me pay! And you know how they are, Stanley and Amy. To them, I am not Stephanie, a woman, a lawyer, a pillar of the Manhattan social scene, the unattainable object of men's wishes. To them, I am still Jenna's roommate, with Roman noodles for lunch and ketchup for dinner, and probably a virgin too."

Stephanie was seated on the recliner at the side of the hospital bed. Her eyes traveled across the soft pastels of the drawings she brought from Jenna's place to soften the harsh tones of this place. Every other day for the last few weeks, she would come here to sit at her friend's side and talk about memories and life. She would make fun of herself and her friend, light to medium to serious and back, talk about her city, her beautiful wounded city. She would talk about work and her community garden, talk about the latest date and her latest culinary discovery.

"Funny," she was thinking in the cab on her way home from another Jenna session. "This helps me as well; it gives me something concrete to concentrate on. It helps me cope and move forward. I am looking at the people around me in the subway, on the street. They all have this look, this 'I will get better' look. And I have my Jenna—my friend Jenna—quietly breathing through her tubes, her numbers, heart rate and blood pressure, oxygen level and synaptic activity registering on the screen in a slow and determined parade."

"I have Jenna and she has me, and just like the crowds in Grand Central station, we shall overcome. We shall pull through. The towers fell, but we will build them again. We are New York, still the best place on earth. And when I waver, when I let the horrors invade my consciousness, there is always the next Jenna day to plan, to tend to, to prepare for, and it does help, a lot."

Startled, she realized that as this was going through her mind, she was describing the dessert to Jenna. Was she on autopilot the whole time?

"…and I'm glad you were not there to talk me out of it," she smiled.

"You should have seen these layers of ice cream, coconut, mint, and my favorite—cookies and cream. I'm telling you, first thing we do when you get out of here is to go there and I will force feed you the stuff; it was superb."

She watched her friend's face for a sign of recognition or an eyelid movement. Lip fluttering. Anything…

Quelling her disappointment for god knows how many times, she continued. "I saw Juan and his sister Karla again yesterday at the garden," she said.

The garden was her newfound joy. Nestled between nondescript city buildings, a patch of greenery owned by the downtown community. Stephanie had to guard the garden once a month for eight hours and in return had a key and could go there whenever she wanted to.

"Who would have thought it?" she thought for the millionth time.

"A pond? Frogs? Goldfish? A freaking gazebo? A pebbled pathway gently curving its way amongst oaks and pine trees? Birds? In Manhattan—in fucking Lower East Side Manhattan?"

This discovery really elevated her neighborhood status in her eyes. If there were ever any chance, she would concede uptown advantages—security, banks, nicer post office—the garden pretty much killed it. The garden and the company.

"I am so happy with this garden, you know. The best thing is not the garden itself, but meeting people I would never meet socially otherwise. Take Karla and Juan; her dream is to become a beautician and he wants to be a baseball player. Seven years old, and they already have their minds all set; now that's beautiful and real. I love these kids. I really do."

A gentle knock on the door startled her a bit—Chris. "You don't have to do that," said Stephanie, as he entered.

They both smiled. They remembered the time when Chris opened the door just when Stephanie was reminiscing about the time Jenna told her about her first night with Chris.

Details and all…

"Clawing at the bed post? Battlefield of pillows and linen? Had to flip the mattress?" "Squirting like there is no tomorrow?" Chris smiled his slow, disarming smile.

"Of course, I had to knock."

They were both thankful for the brief comic relief, as always gathering strength from each other's presence.

He knows the answer but feels compelled to ask anyway. "Anything?"

"Nope," says Stephanie. Like a dark cloud, her worries about Jenna—momentarily lifted by the memory parade settled back in her being, making their presence felt. His hand caressed her shoulder in a lovely gesture of friendliness.

Stephanie's eyes watered a bit. To hide it, she punched him playfully.

"Her body is not cold yet, and you are already hitting on me? Keep your hands to yourself, Mister!"

They locked eyes, drawing solace from each other. "Go," he said. "Get some rest. I am good here."

Stephanie nodded and left. As she closed the door behind her, she could see him stretching his long legs over a chair, ready for a long shift. Stephanie was momentarily comforted by his presence next to her friend; it was as if a part of her was still there.

*****

The voices seemed to recede a bit now. "Is she sitting with Chris on his balcony looking at Prospect Park? Are they making the grocery list for the afternoon picnic? Is Stephanie there or was she going to join them later?"

They never knew if Stephanie would come solo or not, always a surprise, always a pleasant one, always with another wonderful observation delivered with sass and spunk.

"What are her parents doing here? Their annual visit was not supposed to be until Christmas. Damn! Is she late for gift shopping?" Jenna always took pride in being ready with the gift list, way ahead of everyone else. She spent months in zany shops

and quaint markets to find this special gift and that special trinket for the upcoming gift season. It was her gift to find the perfect gift. Anything that threw her off her stride could not be tolerated. She would often get extra items, as she knew Stephanie would fall behind and panic sometime in mid-December and Jenna would come to the rescue.

It was fun rescuing her friend, but not as much fun as teasing her about it.

"So what are they doing here? Chris, did you know that they were coming?" Chris doesn't listen. He is apparently busy with his model airplane, such a strange kick for a grown man, a MAN's man. Jenna liked her men to be men, no metrosexuals for her. And yet, Chris would be found sometimes hunched over his beloved collection, immune to her barbs, flashing his smile and silencing her with a kiss.

But no, this wasn't Chris, nor was it Stephanie, nor her parents. It wasn't even the guys from the office. Who was talking? About what and what were they saying?

Some words reached her ears. She tried to concentrate. Something was odd, very odd. "What was that voice? Temple? Silver? Talking about silver? And blood? Was it a trip? What was she on?" She couldn't remember what she took. Maybe something broke?

Things did get a little out of hand in these parties. It was worth the feeling though, even worth the disapproving look from Stephanie. "Damn it, Girl. I need some outlet. I am Jenna, always planned, always prepared, always have the answers and the questions, always doing the job. I do need to let go sometimes."

"But what am I saying? I have been out of that for a long time now. This was years ago. I stopped the drugs when I started the new job. That's right. It is Stephanie, telling me about my going-clean party. She dragged me to this downtown café, I remember, dirty tablecloth, peeling wallpaper in the women's room. Oh Stephanie. Couldn't we do it here? Where it is nice and clean."

"What was that about horses? And ships? What's with the swords-and-sandals imagery? I am trying, but I can't place it. I want to listen, but it all gets mixed up. I think I am going to call in sick. I had a very productive week and I could use the rest. Maybe my uncle will visit. I haven't seen him in a long time. Did

he call? Email? I think he did, but I can't quite place it. Am I supposed to meet Stephanie after work for another match?"

"I did lose the one yesterday and I hate losing to her. I swear, sometimes I...I love her to death, but it does seem unfair that after swallowing a double quarter-pounder with bacon and cheese, she can still beat me. Chris...it is Chris's fault. Chris and his new moves, pinning me down, making it last so long. So why am I hearing these voices and where do they come from?"

"Is it morning? Am I waking up? From what dream and to what dream? Lights! Sounds!"

"Too strong!!! Too strong!!! Too strong!!!"

Everything blurs, then gets louder and louder.

"Make it stop! Make it stop! Make it stop!!!!"

*****

Now the archon ... has three names. The first name is Yaltabaoth, the second is Saklas ('fool'), and the third is Samael. And he is impious in his arrogance which is in him. For he said, "I am God and there is no other God beside me," ... He is Demiurge ... but as a ray of light from above enters the body of man and gives him a soul, Yaldabaoth is filled with envy ... At the consummation of all things all light will return to the Pleroma. But Yaldabaoth, the Demiurge, with the material world, will be cast into the lower depths.

Apocryphon of John circa 120–180 AD

He is an archon with the face of a lion, half flame, and half-darkness.

Pistis Sophia

Chapter 4

Imagine a dark tunnel.

Darker.

Darker still.

Now imagine its depth; darkness wrapped in darkness, deep, bottomless.

Deeper.

It goes so deep that it defies the eye trying to perceive the reach of the darkness.

The darkness conveys a sense of distorted reality. It is as if where it leads cannot be put in words; strange, but there it is.

At the top, it is just a tunnel, with all the trappings of a man-made tunnel combined with years of treatment by the indifferent hand of nature. The word nature may hint of something NATURAL, but the hand of nature here is anything but devolving, decaying, destructive.

This is not the hand of a graceful Mother Nature, nor lively vegetation or majestic mountain ranges, lilting birdcalls, or lush, rich soil sinking slightly under your feet. It does not have a welcoming beach with soft pink sand and a gentle breeze. It does not even have the harsh beauty and raw primal power of ancient desert vistas; vistas filled with the terrible awesomeness of giant rocks and boulders, echoing with timeless energy and tales of past glorious generations dwarfing the occasional human gazing upon them with their ageless symphony of stone and soil.

There is none of that here, none of that.

The hand of nature you should picture is a twisted, harsh, underground force—an urban nature—inherently contradictory by definition. And yet here it is, strong, overwhelming, gruesome. Its overpowering force is so heavy it seems to take its toll not only on the view but also on the viewer.

This translates into heaps of abandoned equipment, parts of machines long forgotten. That are half-covered by even more ancient parts, half covered in dust, mold, and a multitude of living and crawling things, and remnants of living and crawling things.

Puddles of liquid that resemble water only by their liquidity are spread here, fallen rocks, mud pits, a rotten and rotting vile hodgepodge of live garbage, dead garbage, and everything-in-between garbage, defying the age-old classification between mineral, vegetable, and animal. Makes it almost impossible to determine where the one ends and the other begins.

And it doesn't stop, oh no.

It goes deeper. It stretches the eyes and the senses. What could be there at the end of that revolting tunnel? How deep does it go?

Sandwiched between a filthy apartment building and a crumpled bodega somewhere in the south Bronx, there is a nondescript metal door locked with a solid-looking, heavy-duty lock. It seems that no one has ever seen that door open.

It was in the dead of night. The block was sealed from the outside by two large sanitation trucks, one at each end of the street. The foreman didn't know why the man that contacted him occasionally wanted that block sealed. All he knew was that he was paid handsomely in cash to sit in his truck and seal this particular block for about four hours once every few months. Meanwhile, a group of men in dark suits and glasses went inside the block and emerged hours later.

He inherited this lucrative post from his mentor, who got it from his. The foreman knew that this particular perk went back a long, long time, back to the horse-drawn carriage garbage collection era sometime in the late 1800s, possibly earlier; it pays, pun intended—to know your history.

He also knew—and some of his teammates paid the price for that knowledge—that it was unwise to try to look, or to figure out where the small group of men were heading on these late-night escapades.

At the mouth of the tunnel, deep below the cars that carried millions of unsuspecting workers to their unremarkable cubicles every day, deep below the humans that attracted the attention of Toth and her book about the mole people, of Brennam and his research, below countless prying eyes and thrill seekers, was the

Village. It was huddled in the dark, slimy slopes and led by one who called himself the Angel of the Dark, the third one of his line.

There he ruled, beyond the reach of the pop culture, of the myth makers, of journalists and writers, of filmmakers and researchers of urban legends, of law enforcement and tax collectors.

The powers that wanted him defended protected his domain. With absolute power, there was absolute defense; with absolute defense came absolute obedience.

His subjects were society's rejects who were beyond homelessness and being mentally ill. They were the total and utter dregs of society. If you wanted to find a stable of people that no one will claim and no one will miss, people who are at your mercy—for the right price—then this was the right place.

Although rumors persisted about the "so called" mole people, they were never substantiated. Did they work? Were they all panhandlers? Thieves? Robbers? Their true source of income remained hidden. The true source of their existence was much darker, buried deep under the depths of the city, buried under the veils of secrecy. The true source was buried under darkness and sudden unexplained deaths.

Only the few that needed to know knew. And they extracted the payment in carefully regulated intervals. Intermittent sacrifices to the god of... The victims didn't even fathom how appropriate this was. Even if they knew, it would do them little good.

For a bargain was struck between the men that came in the dead of night and the village. Money changed hands and the selected disposable humans were loaded into the back of the vehicle that stood there waiting.

It was suggested that the timing of the building of underground trains in the world's largest cities was somehow coordinated, that somehow it all happened almost at once, that it was no coincidence. The truth?

Truth could be in short supply at times, the men knew. They knew that the truth lay safely hidden under miles of rock and soil. They reveled in the knowledge and in what was about to transpire under all those miles.

If you were there in the vehicle speeding down to the abyss you wouldn't last long. As the distance and the depth grew, it seemed that the darkness grew darker and darker until it seemed to thicken and become tangible, pushing down on the moving silhouette. It was no longer familiar darkness. As vile as the pit was in the first phase of this vile journey, it was still of human touch, albeit that most humans would not want to touch.

But down there, all was forgotten. Only the TOUCHING darkness was pouring into the consciousness of the men in the dark suits. Thick, mental fog started to form in their minds' eyes, slowly materializing and filling them with vivid real-time memories and sensations of every imaginable and unimaginable human suffering. It was as if ghosts of public execution…of quartering…of inquisition chambers…being scalped alive…gas chambers…rape and slaughter…axes chopping limbs of men…of women…of children…of infants, of victims being buried alive, covered with snakes, spiders, and rats, merging their unspeakable agony directly, intimately with the travelers minds.

They were thrown into the gaping salivating mouths of lions like the ancient Christians in Nero's Rome. They were nailed to a sharpened stake as in Prince Vlad Dracula's garden, cut down limb by limb as in the most exquisite Chinese torture. It was as if all possible ways that men so painstakingly developed over the eons to inflict pain, suffering, death and worse, on each other were represented in that proud, merciless, symphonic poem of agony and horror.

All of these visions were shrieking their terrified screams into the consciousness of the travelers. It would have made any ordinary human stop before their brains turned into mush or were incinerated from the inside. They would reverse course and run for their lives, or simply go mad and allow themselves to be dragged into the depths of this hell by the convulsing ghosts into sharing their endless horror.

It was a hell of ten thousand deaths by ten thousand killers, all with a deep background of joy and satisfaction emanating from a mind that was watching all this misery with immense pleasure. Its cruelty superseded all other cruelty in this demonic gallery, in this dark garden of wicked and horrible flowers.

This was the defense around the perimeter of the force that dwelled at the bottom of the pit. It would destroy anyone that came within its grasp, unless the visitor had already allowed the darkness in. There were only a few ways, and they were known only to the few.

Those in the box—the offering—were already drugged to allow them passage through the walls of horror.

We are conditioned to think that evil deeds—violent and despicable acts—are committed for a purpose, vile though the purpose may be. But what if the act *is* the purpose?

Books and scholars tell us that there are no evil men or evil deeds; that when men commit evil, these men believe they are doing good. We are told that Hitler loved his country, that Genghis Khan was a free spirit, that Caligula wanted to restore Roman glory, that Stalin was standing for the oppressed…

This theory has no standing here.

It is there at the bottom of the pit, where darkness let them through, that the delegation finally arrived. They rode in a vehicle that seemed to hover above the liquid, whispering darkness and moved with arrogant elegance. The passengers sat at the front. The big box rested on the back.

They were allowed in.

If they were petrified, they hid it well.

Inside the vault was a dark black and purple hall. Chairs rounded a velvet-covered Circle in the center of the large cavern. There were symbols on the velvet cover. The symbols changed, first at a rate too quick for the human eye to recognize the symbol. And then, too quick for the human eye to recognize the change, and finally, too quick for the human eye to recognize the rate of change. Every once in a while, an image would form. At times, it was a drawing, and at times, it seemed to become three-dimensional: the body of a serpent, the face of a lion. Then the flickering would resume.

The box was carried out and opened. It contained a boy and a girl in homeless rags. The innocent faces provided a stark contrast with the sinister purpose that permeated the vast chamber. Their torn clothing exposed patches of pale skin and skinny limbs, silent witnesses to the life they lived in the dark village.

Their eyes were vacant and empty. They stood there, their sweet features covered with the dirt of their daily existence. The girl even had an orange stain on her left cheek, a remnant of a candy bar foraged from the subway station. It left its sweet kiss on her little face before she went back to her very own private Golgotha.

And don't think for a second that this went unnoticed. For the powers in that place, they had quite a knack for details. After all, in details lies perfection and total satisfaction. What was that old saying—the devil is in the details? If only those who used it so freely and carelessly up there in the human world knew its true origin, meaning, and purpose…

After a subtle smile curled his thick lips, the tallest man spoke, aiming his words at the center of the velvet-covered circle, where the flickering was occurring.

"An alarm has been sounded."

The cover seemed to change the pace of the symbol flickering, as if in response. The serpent image—like the smile of the Cheshire cat—was moving in and out of visibility.

"We have been summoned and we came with the offering." The Circle resumed its flickering.

The man turned his head.

"Did you secure the transaction?"

"It was completed First Archon," said the man to his left. "Good. Let's get to it then."

The other men removed the velvet cover. It covered nothing.

Or so it seemed, just vast blackness. Was it just dark matter? Was it a hole leading to mind-bending distances? Was there something pulsating in the darkness? How far down did it extend? Where did it lead? One couldn't tell, and neither could the occupants of the room. All they knew was that at a terrible cost, this was their source of power, of wealth, of life and of death.

The homeless children stepped out of the box. Their eyes were open but bereft of the life force that provides character and recognition to our facial features, which makes us human and without which we become just animated objects. These objects could be turned into subjects of the entire range of human experience in an apparent contradiction of the human/non-human nature of what was about to transpire.

"Stop," said the tall man.

He stepped forward and gently lifted both boy's and girl's chins so his shade-covered gaze would penetrate deep into their souls. His finger delicately caressed the orange stain on the little girl's cheek. After all, he did have grand plans. He had a good teacher and he wanted to surprise that teacher one day, to surprise, to surpass.

"Here," he said, handing each one a chocolate-covered cherry. The cherries were laced with more of what made the children docile, in order to increase the looming effect. He had learned long ago that ceremony played a big role here. He learned that the more the contrast between the input and the output, the greater the reward.

The same is true in all business, you buy cheap and sell dear, in business and in pleasure. Only this was business and pleasure combined, albeit those words carry a special meaning here, way beyond their everyday, mundane meaning, their one of a kind meaning for the well-to-do and even way beyond the selected few who THOUGHT they had business and pleasure cornered. They wouldn't last a second here, in this chamber.

The children munched on their offering, lifeless eyes still fixated on the tall man. An altar rose from the blackness behind them, forming out of the menacing darkness.

Stairs from opposite sides of the black Circle were stretching to the altar. As if commanded, the children, with their chocolate-stained hands and cheeks, started stepping toward the altar. The boy came from the right, the girl from the left. Their motion was at an *adagio* pace, ceremonial and thoughtful.

It was as if the force that was guiding the event made certain that every second would count. And each second did count for it was feeding time; a rare, delicious, special, and hard-to-come-by delicacy in this new world order that the power was fighting. Order that unfortunately left little room ahead of the flesh-craving darkness, the power was adapting though, as it always had.

Only several twitching hands and a few lips being slowly licked marred the impassiveness of the men in the Circle… After all, they were allowed their fun as well, as long as they did not distract from the main event.

When the children reached their target, suddenly the masks fell; they were just two terrified children.

Their cries and pleas for help were the aperitif. Shrieks of horror echoed through the large room as an apparition rose from the deep.

Serpent body and lion face—it seemed to grow, to materialize, first into full shape and then into more than full shape, as if its reality was more real than reality itself.

Then, it moved back into solidity and less than solidity. The creature was playing its own scale of existence with arrogant power and total disdain of the rules of normal nature.

It was hard to see beyond the thickening anaconda-like entity, but hearing seemed to take on a new meaning. Soon, the pleas for help changed into screams of torment. What was taking place inside this Circle defied visual description but was *felt* by all watching.

The men watched silently. The light and dark, red and black, danced inside the lenses of their dark glasses. Could the little bodies tolerate so much pain?

Severing body parts and re-attaching them in the wrong order? Skinning one child to cover the other? Forcing the little figures to collide into one monstrosity?

It was hard to determine what was exactly happening inside the beyond-death hug of the semi-solid creature that engulfed the small-form humans. It was difficult but not impossible.

Finally, it ended. There was a feeling of immense satisfaction emanating from inside the Circle. Pieces of discarded bodies were scattered about—a tooth, an ear, a finger—caught inside the now seemingly inert, yet strangely solid darkness. Only a hint of the lion-faced serpent was hovering in its own dimension, adjacent to this one.

A voice spoke, a beautiful seductive voice, "Once more, you have proven your worth, Gonar." The tall man bowed slightly.

"At your service, O Holy One."

"Do you know why you are here? Why you had to wake me up on this day?" A familiar smile twisted the man's full lips.

"Since things were going so well lately, we were hoping the day would be near. But then we heard that a 36 alarm had been activated, and we knew the time had come to commune with our god yet again."

The voice sounded pleased.

"Indeed. And a very powerful alarm it is; not in centuries has this alarm rung." "Where?"

"When?"

Questions echoed around the room and then the Circle was emanating rays of what looked like plasma. The men were all hit by those rays. It seemed to be painful and the presence in the Circle seemed to revel in yet another experience of its vast power of destruction and complete control of its subjects, the useless and the useful.

Two of the men fell, their shades broken into shards of glass. It was as if two tiny grenades went off inside their eyelids; blood was seeping from their eye sockets; soon, they were still. The rest composed themselves. Never mind the fallen; they will be discarded. There were plenty of replacements waiting in the wings, the best and brightest of society, through endless layers of rituals and secret shell organizations. Skull and Bones, Freemasons, Illuminati, 456, Golden Dawn, Harmetists, Rosicrucians, Ordo, Templars, the Bilderberg Group…politicians. lawyers, captains of industry. Words were whispered; sweet poison on poised ears, in boardrooms, in the splendor of the world's largest mansions. In power centers and secret vaults. In pleasure palaces and torture chambers. Words will be whispered, words of unlimited power, unlimited wealth, unlimited…simply UNLIMITED.

It was no wonder that they did not pay attention to the fallen. They would be easily replaced.

"Just a quick reminder of who I am and who you are," said the seductive voice. "Unexpected yet welcome additional treat," was written all over the oily satisfaction dripping from every syllable.

"Now you know almost all you need to know. When the time is right, you will bring her to me, alive and unspoiled."

"And when will the time be right?" asked Gonar.

The blackness of the Circle seemed to crawl at him, but he was unperturbed, committed. It was not the first time the Circle had tested him. There was a strange symbiosis between man and power. Both seem to tread on the verge of confrontation. Perhaps this was the way it ought to be in this twisted world, away from light, away from humanity, away and yet so close.

Perhaps that was why Gonar was still standing. His was the longest reign in a long line of slain ancestors.

"It is a delicate matter," mused the voice, seduction and anticipation mixed.

"There is a lot at stake here. If I have her like I had these two morsels you fed me, it would be a wondrous revenge on my archenemies."

A pause—the air seemed to thicken even more.

"But, if I am able to penetrate even deeper, I could do more, much more. I could change that cursed balance of holy darkness and cursed light. I could…sever their link of refuge. It may very well be the one that was prophesized and if it is, I could… I could…"

The Lion/serpent seemed to grow bigger and to make everything else grow smaller. Was it emitting newfound strength or was it rekindled from the previous epoch? Was it really happening? Were they all about to be crushed under this monster? There were frightened looks around the chamber as men stepped backward, but not their leader.

Not Gonar.

Gonar felt exalted. He knew, of course, of the prophecy. Like all his ancestors, he was well educated and indoctrinated in this holy fight they all shared. Like all his ancestors, he was hoping it would happen in his lifetime and he waited. He waited a long, long time.

Luke, I am your father!

Darth Vader, Star Wars

Chapter 5

"Make it stop!"

Stephanie woke up from her daze. Incredibly, unexpectedly, Jenna was staring at her. Her eyes were open! Pale eyes inside pale face, surrounded by pale sheets. All the paleness seemed to emphasize the terror in her eyes, fear-stricken yet unfocused eyes...

Eyes open! Eyes filled with terror! Eyelids wildly flailing about! There was no recognition in the eyes, no comprehension of the surroundings, nothing except the terror.

Stephanie came back to her senses, stood up, almost fell and steadied herself, and rushed to the bed.

"Jenna, you are awake!!!"

"Make it stop!!! It hurts. Make it stop!!!" Jenna's body was hurled from side to side. Convulsions shook her uncontrollably. Eyes staring at something only Jenna could see.

"Jenna!!!" Stephanie was at her side, clutching her friend's shoulder, suddenly very afraid, not the fear that she learned to live with, but an immediate, Oh-my-god-she-is-out-of-her-mind-she-is-going-to-die of fear...

She pressed harder, fighting whatever it was that was controlling her friend. "Jenna!!!"

As if in response, the yelling stopped, Jenna's body lost its rigid contortions, sagged back to the familiarity of hospital-issued pillowcases.

"They were, they are...it stopped, it finally stopped..." she was gasping.

"Jenna," Stephanie wasn't sure if the alarm was over. She was readying herself for...

And then, Jenna's eyes came into focus, into recognition.

"Stephanie! What are you doing..." her eyes started to see around herself.

"…here?"

"Where am I?"

"What am I doing here?" "What…?"

Stephanie was now on the bed next to her, careful, not to upset the tubes.

Something told Stephanie to be quiet, patient, to allow Jenna her own pace of facing reality; her new reality.

"Am I in a…hospital? Why? What happened?" asked Jenna in a tiny voice. Stephanie couldn't answer, not yet.

Jenna slowly noticed the sheer look of gratitude and joy on her friend's face. It washed away that unexplained fear that made her yell for it to stop earlier, whatever it was.

It took away the unexplained terror that seized her senses just seconds ago in terrified consciousness and for an eternity before, inside her private, inner self.

Stephanie's eyes were wet. In a noble effort to be true to her I-don't-give-a-damn-persona, she tried and failed to hide them.

She gave up, watching the calm, efficient manner of the hospital nurses that came in. Stephanie was now standing alongside the bed. For once, she was thankful that she had these first precious few seconds with Jenna before strangers came in. For once, she was thankful that the staff was a bit slow to respond. She was thankful that she alone could see Jenna come back, to see the mindless terror turning into loving recognition in her eyes.

She leaned in. Nurses staying gracefully out of her way, adjusting tubes and sheets, exchanging remarks and writing in charts in muffled voices; allowing the friends their moment of intimacy.

"Jenna," she whispered. "Oh, Jenna, you have no idea…so glad to have you back."

"Back," Jenna asked, still weak and confused but visibly drawing strength from her friend's presence. "How long has it been?" And she knew before Stephanie answered that it was a long, long time.

"Was I…?"

Stephanie nodded. As the nurses were gently removing her from near the bed to perform their duty, Jenna was looking into her friend's eyes. Her eyes filled with questions, just as they were filled with terror moments ago. Stephanie smiled; she had a long story to tell.

In the days and weeks that followed, Jenna, like her city, was getting slowly back to some semblance of normalcy. It was very strange to attend all these memorial services. To feel grateful that she wasn't there in the burning inferno, in the death trap that once was the world's most celebrated hub.

She still didn't quite know how it happened. Short-term memory loss, said Doctor Martin. Jenna learned to appreciate his calm and calculated way of communicating, punctuated by occasional bursts of warmth. After all, she was a patient. Jenna hated being a patient in the few times she had had health issues. This time, with this doctor, she actually didn't mind. She wanted very badly to get to the bottom of what happened. The silver lining was that the interaction between doctor and patient was actually a pleasant one, small miracles and all that.

They had multiple conversations. And it seemed that right around that fateful day, the day that would forever be burned into the heart of New York, right there is where she had her lapse that had ended in her being in a coma. Her boss remembered her calling in sick the night before, but she didn't. Her phone records confirmed that.

She didn't remember screaming, breaking furniture or any of these other events described to her by a concerned super and less concerned and more annoyed neighbors. Park Avenue had limited tolerance for that sort of behavior after all. Jenna had to get used to thinly veiled judgmental looks from the snooty ladies in the apartment across the hall as they were walking their pride and joy—two Shih Tzu dogs attired with matching (of course!) topcoats. Her positive mind found some humor in that. It was as if those looks came straight out of an O. Henry story.

The staff was displaying a mix of concern for her and concern for the building's reputation. At times, she felt she just wanted to forget it all and move on with her life. But even when she felt like this, she knew she would never be able to actually forget.

No way, no fucking way.

In the hours and days, it took to restore her apartment to her favorite combination of calmness, quiet elegance, and comfort, she kept wondering why it all happened. Why did she flip like that? It was an odd feeling. Searching inside her mind like a little girl going to the attic with a flashlight, looking for unknown content in unknown boxes, more than slightly afraid of what would emerge when the lid opened.

Could she find a clue? Could she unearth a piece of evidence? Anything? It was so NOT like her. Everything in its place; neatly explained and categorized. This was her motto, order in order, order in disorder, everything regimented, serious and silly, nutrition and guilty pleasures (when no one else was watching). Jenna reveled in having her world exactly the way she wanted it. "This wasn't right!!!"

She wanted to scream.

"This wasn't right at all! I don't deserve this!"

It seemed to be that. She was very much like New York in this way. And just like New York, she was searching for answers to the unexpected tragic events that threw woman and city into a limbo of uncertainty and contemplation.

Even the drugs she took or the fantasy books she read before were regimented as well. They were a lightning rod, a diversion. Not an escape into forged reality when real reality couldn't be faced, as so many around her craved with their fantasies and game consoles, not Jenna. A momentary sedative, nothing more, nothing less!

Jenna never needed to escape; she enjoyed her world—right up until 9/11.

Then came the doubts again, assailing her senses in a way that never happened to her before. Looking at her mental mirror, she was wondering…

Perhaps Stephanie was right, she was sometimes thinking. Perhaps all that order finally caught up with me. But she was half joking with me, wasn't she?

Could Stephanie be right? No way. No way!

The recent unexplained events were powerful but not powerful enough to shake her core. No, this wasn't it. Her system still works. She will just have to be patient; perhaps the coma will never be explained. Perhaps it is better not explained. Perhaps learning to live with one vast unexplained event in her life would help her continue being who she is, the exception that proves the rule. After all, SOMETHING made her stay home and the same something may have plunged her into the coma; it was logical to assume that.

Jenna was a creature of logic and she did, at times, assume that she should therefore be thankful, shouldn't she? She should be thankful for being here and not incinerated in the burning tower, should she not?

But then again, Jenna was a creature of logic, right? New York City was never attacked by plane. Jenna Berg was never in a coma. And yet, both city and Jenna had their mutual traumatic event on the same exact day. There HAD to be a connection, had to!

Or was she completely out of her mind for thinking that? Was she?

All of this was cycling in her mind as life slowly began to fill the void, to soothe the agony of not knowing. At times, it seemed almost back to regular scheduled programming, but at times, it seemed…

It seemed…

It was as if someone or something had interrupted her life and was pulling her back into doubt. Whenever the clouds of doubt were starting to disperse, she felt like she could almost make peace with *her* own private battle with 9/11.

As if someone or something made a decision, not her decision. As if she was ACTIVATED (or deactivated, depending on the mood she was in when thinking about all of this) as if…

Back and forth, back and forth.

"I'm telling you, I keep feeling that any moment now, someone or something will jump behind me and yell boo!" she said.

"Boo!" said Stephanie to the receiver, making Jenna laugh. "Seriously."

"Seriously what? Maybe even imperial Jenna is not able to unlock all the mysteries of the universe, girl! You should stop obsessing and start living again. Chris tells me it has been weeks since he last stayed over."

"Look at you guys, gossiping like old women."

Stephanie laughed. "Give us some gossip, Jenna. Come on, let's see what you got. It has been a long time since this Chica had some good stuff to pass on."

Stephanie listened with pleasure to the short burst of laughter on the other end; laughter was in short supply lately.

A few seconds of comfortable silence, the kind of silence that, if you are lucky, you can find a few people to share it with. Lots can be transmitted with this kind of silence, trust, friendship, strength.

When Jenna was very young and very serious about her music lessons, her teacher used to remind her about the power of silence in music. She took that power from the score page to her pages of life and with Stephanie, those silences were cherished and respected, shared and appreciated like this one.

"Listen, Stephanie," said Jenna, back in talk mode. "You know me, I need to know. I always need to know."

Stephanie heard that tone and went into her firewall mode.

"Hey, why don't you come over tonight? I swear I will even make a salad."

Jenna smiled. "You? A salad? You must think I lost more than short term memory…"

"Hey, I'm trying to be nice, would you rather some hot wings, onion rings, and jalapeno peppers?"

Jenna squirmed for an answer.

"I thought so, come eightish. It will give me time to get some—vegetables," uttering the word in a way that brought yet another smile to Jenna's lips.

"Till tomorrow."

"Till tomorrow."

Somewhere else, another phone clicked its punctuation.

This time, it was different. There were more boxes and more lives were spent; the Circle was expanding. This was the time for action, not just for words. For the Circle had to have dominion over all that is, as it did in times long forgotten; destroying everyone and everything that stood in its path.

For the alarm was signaling, strong and promising; a hope that lay dormant for generations was now awakened. A narrow window was about to be opened.

And only the Circle knew the extent of the planning and plotting that would lead to the ultimate goal that lay in the future. Nothing, however, prevented it from enjoying the process and the elation of its servants. After all, it was the giver of all that should be enjoyed by the lucky, selected few… It was times to advance, to ascend.

Finally, when the screaming subsided, the remnants were discarded.

The men could see that deep inside the Circle, depth that defied their eyes and froze their thought, something was forming; something was rising.

It was a sphere, a large sphere, almost transparent; markings on the sphere were familiar. As the sphere materialized, it looked more and more like a giant globe. And then, inside the sphere, at its exact center, something started to rotate, quicker and quicker. As the rotation grew, the dimension grew, a pitch was sounding, higher and higher, faster and faster, larger and larger.

The men around the Circle removed their glasses. You could see that the same rotation was happening in their eyes.

Faster.

Louder.

Bigger.

And then, the head of the sphere burst open and the rotation was set loose, like a serpent raising its head, back and forth, to and fro. The snake head, lion-faced, the real force behind the images seen before was gathering momentum. As the rotation speed almost made it disappear from the visual spectrum, visible only to the men and their rotating eyes, it burst out of the cavern, into the tunnel and into the night.

"Follow," said the voice. "Follow and remember, this has to be done the right way, the ancient way. Your reward awaits."

Stephanie was walking to the supermarket in Union Square; normally, she didn't shop there. It was out of her 'comfort zone'. "This may be the biggest reason why I live here," she used to say to guests visiting from the outside. "We have it all without needing a car."

"Show me another place with a 24/7 subway, and I will grudgingly acknowledge that there may be other places as good as this one."

However, if she was going to make Jenna some semi-healthy food, she might as well make an event out of it and make it all the way to 14th Street, Whole Foods, where white people shop, she smiled.

She could make herself go there, just this once…

She enjoyed the walk, looking at store windows, catching conversations. Her city was coming back little by little. There were constant reminders—candlelight vigils on sidewalks, walls covered with pictures of loved ones perished, and a heightened security presence. The city *was* coming back though, and Stephanie thought that Jenna was coming back as well.

And just like her beloved city, Jenna's recovery was slow, fragile, and prone to setbacks. You never knew when she would get that distant look on her face. You never knew when her tentative grasp on reality would feel like it was slipping, scaring the bejesus out of Stephanie, prompting crude jokes about calories, cattiness, Jewishness and male genitalia, all in an effort for a pale smile to break through the clouds of doubts and despair. The city was the same, made you want to step on the gas a few years into the future, thought Stephanie. Out of this…this state of VICTIMIZATION. "And some of us walk like we deserve it," Stephanie was sometimes thinking. "Like it was some kind of punishment or something."

"Some form of American guilt, feeling guilty for being successful, of shame, being ashamed for being who we are, of who WE ARE? Never! Never in a million years!"

This really focused her anger, and she felt justified, strengthened. A sense of empowerment engulfed her. She was smiling. A sense of confidence, helping her friend AND her city, what could be better? Caring seemed to fit well into her usual casualness.

True, Jenna is the one that pointed out that 'broken-winged bird' syndrome in her best friend. Jenna is the one that used to mock Stephanie on her tendency to collect those broken-winged souls to nurture and protect, from men with serious intimacy and communication issues to those kids in the garden, buying candy and magazines from the old corner store on Houston Street, the store that seemed to be empty all the time.

That candy was seriously decrepit, chocolate bars from the Carter administration.

Stuff you'd buy and throw away; yes, Stephanie was indeed guilty of that.

Jenna would point that out and Stephanie, in defense of her too-cool-for-school reputation, would deny it half seriously.

Now that Jenna was the object of all this nurturing, there was no more denial.

Stephanie mused on all of this as she was passing the clatter of Indian restaurants on 6th Street. "Perhaps I am changing as well. Perhaps there is a silver lining here, beyond 9/11, beyond Jenna. Maybe this is what growing up feels like; don't know if I like it…"

She was passing a Rite Aid and heading towards the supermarket, when all of a sudden, she missed a step, lost her balance, and almost fell. It was as if someone or something had shoved her forward violently, but there was no one around. Her heart was beating fast for a moment. She felt lightheaded, that sort of lightheadedness you feel when you step off a treadmill after a run, or maybe that sort of rush that you feel when you just move too fast. (Not that Stephanie was ever accused of moving too fast or frequently stepping off a treadmill after a run).

She recoiled, still breathing hard and looked around. The people around her just kept walking, minding their own business.

"God bless New Yorkers," she was thinking. You can always count on them to ignore you at embarrassing moments.

She was steadying herself when her head suddenly jerked to one side. For a moment, she just stood there and then, her body turned but in a strange way. She headed back to the Rite Aid; for a very brief moment, the rotating in her eyes was visible before she cast them down to the floor as she entered the store.

"What's with the shades?" asked Jenna as she walked in the door. She hadn't been here in a while and wanted to check out what was new in her friend's apartment. Seeing Stephanie with dark glasses was only somewhat surprising as Stephanie was known to go on different kicks every once in a while, like the time she decided to have a feather in her hair or that god-awful nose ring Jenna convinced her to get rid of.

"Why pimple your face, Girl; didn't you have enough pimples in junior high?"

"Oh, nothing important," said Stephanie. "Just trying out a new look." She was slurring her words a bit. Jenna looked at her, a bit puzzled.

"Are you OK? I am the one who is recovering from a near-death experience, remember?" Stephanie managed a smile, not the best one, but it passed inspection.

"Well, what are we having for dinner?" asked Jenna. "It does smell good."

Before Stephanie could answer, the doorbell rang. "Are we expecting more company?" asked Jenna.

Stephanie looked confused, as much as you can look confused when your eyes are not showing.

"No, no, it is probably a neighbor asking for something; you know what it's like down here. Give me a minute."

"Sure, I'm going to hit the bathroom."

Jenna always liked visiting Stephanie's bathroom. When she was growing up, books were not allowed in the bathroom and she got in trouble more than once sneaking books in under her shirt. Stephanie had a nice little library in her bathroom, books that Jenna usually didn't come across, romance novels, house design. She would always spend a few extra minutes here.

About five minutes later, somewhat surprised that Stephanie didn't give her the usual hard time for staying in the john for too long, Jenna emerged from the bathroom and walked to the kitchen.

When she turned at the door, she saw Stephanie… Stephanie was lying down on the floor and…

There was a MAN crouching over her, she could only see his back.

Before anything could happen, before she could scream, faint, recall any of her Krav Maga training or anything else, the man turned around. All the synaptic activity that blazed through her body in extreme emergency mode, in pure adrenalin rush, just froze.

As did she…

And then, a weak "Uncle…Josh?" escaped her lips.

For it was her uncle, crouching next to her best friend's inert body, here in Stephanie's apartment, Josh, who went MIA for a long time, from before…

Jenna felt she was losing her grasp of reality, 'not again' was echoing in her shocked mind. Once again, before anything else could happen, he was at her side, easing her to a chair.

There was a bottleneck of questions in her mind, on her lips, in her eyes…

"What…where…how…Stephanie." Here, this was an immediate one, didn't require her to go very far.

"Stephanie—what happened to her? Is she OK?"

Josh smiled his old reassuring smile.

"She will be fine, she will wake up, have a bit of a headache and that's all."

"But, but…what happened to her? Did she pass out? Like me? Am I contagious?"

"No, Jenna, no. I'm telling you she will be fine."

Josh turned his attention back to Stephanie. He didn't look like he was exactly helping her. The oddity of the way he surveyed the situation would have alarmed Jenna. But she was busy, fighting her private fight with a reality that once again seemed determined to assail her fragile sense of recovered self.

Then she collected herself.

She tried to get out of the chair, to go to her friend, to see what was wrong…

Legs are failing her, she steadies herself against the edge of the table.

In a swift motion, surprising in its agility for a man his age, Josh is next to her, hands on her arms, a specific and familiar touch, where does she remember it from?

"Here, Little One"—his name for her from a long time ago. "Drink this," he offers her a flask.

She manages a pale smile.

"Really, Uncle, I didn't know you were into that stuff."

Josh smiles back.

"It's not what you think, medicinal, not recreational," faint smile, even now she is capable of appreciating his precise and efficient way of communicating.

The moment passes.

"But Stephanie…" she starts again.

"I told you." His reassuring voice resonated close in her ear, soothing her. "She will be OK. Now drink."

Jenna took a small sip. It was warm and soothing, with a bit of a dusty, earthy feel. *Some kind of herbal tea?*

She wasn't quite ready for the sudden hot flush that assailed her senses for a brief interval, aided by her uncle? Abetted by his hands that were still clutching hers?

What was there to see if you happened to be present?

Perhaps you would see how images of the two humans are paraded across the visible spectrum from ultra to infra, how visual information gets distorted and flickers in and out of the same spectrum, completely unreliable. Or perhaps you would have seen focus adjustment on mundane items—window, flowers in a vase, dust bunnies in the corner; it was after all Stephanie's apartment…bookcases changing colors? What was that? Doorknob starting to turn? Perhaps you would have seen a door caving in? Men in dark suites pouring into the room? Screeching to a halt in front of Stephanie's inert body. Hands twitching with immense frustration, hands like claws, like talons, like alligator jaws narrowly missing their prey, men emitting primal noises, from before predators, from before prey, conduits to their remote, crimson monstrosity of a master.

Or perhaps you would have seen nothing, loyal senses betrayed by treacherous reality, a bad combination. As bandwidth and spectrum frequency finalized their intimate dance, Jenna felt her senses oscillating between announcing their betrayal of her consciousness and performing the mental equivalent of a shoulder shrug.

"What was…"

She steadied herself, releasing her hands from his grip, standing, slightly unstable still,

"…that?"

He read more questions in her eyes, and then they receded a bit, "Good."

"Just an old family recipe, it will make you feel better. Come, we have to get going, now."

She looked at him with mild surprise.

"What's the rush and where are we going and…" she pointed towards the floor. "What about Steph? We can't just leave her here!"

He looked at her with a long look and she felt as if he were answering. Jenna was not quite sure what was going on, which ordinarily would drive her insane. But at that moment, she found herself following him outside.

She was following him as she used to when he took her to the library or to the park, eons ago. If she noticed subtle things around her that were out of the ordinary, she didn't point them out. Her sense of self seemed gently wrapped in some sort of mental goose down.

Oddly balancing strangeness and comfort, her trained mind seemed to hit the bars of the reality around her in a different way than usual. But it was also as if someone else was thinking and Jenna was watching with mild interest; the drink, must have been the drink, good.

Jenna found her mind relaxing at that thought, more than it had been for quite a while, also good. Her logical self was deriving comfort from the knowledge that, at least this time, there was a plausible explanation to the way she felt, the way she was experiencing her own brand of reality.

They were in his car.

"Wait a minute, I didn't know you got a new car," she said, feeling the new luxurious leather with sleepy fingers.

"It has been a while," he agreed, driving with speed and skill, and looking at the rear-view mirror; late warning signs were always to be watched for.

All seemed clear and he afforded himself a sigh of relief. A lot of energy was spent on close calls such as this one, this he knew.

"Hey, look," Jenna said, pointing at a street sign. "The new signs are up. I didn't think they would stick to the schedule, what with the attack and all, they do look cool." "Yes, they do," said Josh.

"Are we going to your place?" she asked. "I miss it. Do you still have the hammock?"

In the darkness of Maya, I mistook the rope for the snake, but that is over, and now I dwell in the eternal home of the Lord.

From the writings of Sikhism

Chapter 6

"So, how did you know where I was and why did we have to leave so quickly and what happened to Stephanie…?" The rest of the questions where cut short as Josh put a restraining hand on her arm.

They were sitting in his hammock. The living room looked different, but the hammock was still there.

"Jenna, I know you have a lot of questions."

She nodded. "I would have had more," she said. "But that drink you gave me; it did something to me, right?"

Josh's eyes changed focus. Is she where she needs to be?

"Jenna, I know you have a lot of questions," he restated. "I do have answers for you, but I also have a question of my own."

"Shoot."

"Do you trust me?"

She turned and looked at him. What an odd question.

"Of course, I do. You are my Uncle Josh. How could I not trust you?"

They look at each other, her bluish green and his brown, a moment of truth, of reassurance, of camaraderie. A good moment, one that will supply strength for what is to come.

Finally, he sighs. He takes a sip from the flask, her questioning eyes following his movement, his hand resting on her shoulder. Questioning eyes, she reasons silently, reason is about to go out the window. He reaches slowly to the back of her neck and the subtle place where flesh meets bone, tracing the brain stem.

His fingers are probing for the 'double P' celebrated spot, where connection and gentle pressure can awake both the pineal and the pituitary glands from their mundane functions. You probably are a bit confused right now from the sudden turn of the narrative into a biology lesson, but rest assured, facts will dance their sweet dance around the sweet logic that we all share. And shortly, biology will just have to follow suit, gloriously down that sweet path now, won't it?

And then, again…

After all, Josh and niece are, above all, practical folk. That and the flask…questions will be answered later. Reassured by her inquisitive yet calm eyes and their open, steady gaze, his fingers hit their target with a firm yet not unkind touch.

His eyes changed their focus again as he finds the right position and Jenna's eyes close.

They remained closed, but her body started to shake. Muffled sounds resonated from her lips, eyes still closed. Josh's forehead became contorted with bulging veins. He struggled to maintain the link, a calculated risk. After all, he could have just told her. But he felt that this specific kind of message needed to be transmitted using a deeper layer of reality, of communication. "All for the cause."

He had to remind himself his tired soul was in gloomy anticipation of what was about to transpire, in apprehension since he knew what he needed to do, what he needed to inflict on his beloved niece, of the absolute truth of it, absolute need for it, absolute cruelty of it.

Jenna jerked herself away from the clutching fingers. It was not easy. In fact, it was quite difficult. But in the difficulty lay the seed of actuality, and of inevitability, of doom.

Eyes opening, beyond all the questions about the absurdity—the impossibility—of what just happened was a terrible sickening feeling of unveiling, of reality.

Sounds emanated from her mouth, muffled, half human, long forgotten sounds from before there was language, from before there was coherent sound, from before that.

Foam appeared. Face muscles contorted in ways unseen, unheard, impossible. Sounds changed pitch and velocity. Very remotely, words were starting on their painful journey upward into the surface of consciousness, of communication, struggling to get out.

Struggle. Struggle.

Finally, they formed:

"It was you!!!" she hissed through the foam.

He braced himself.

Afterward, she was spent.

All the energy that was hidden under the bliss of the memory loss, all the rage she felt knowing that she could have prevented it. All that fury caused her to nearly destroy her apartment. The clear as midday memory of her shock, horror, and out-of-this world anger upon rushing in front of the TV screen. The tranquility of a morning snack and New York Times front page shattered to pieces by the TV emergency signal, by the fire truck's sirens. She could remember rushing to watch, to hear with unbelieving ears, to watch with unbelieving eyes, to remember the email with unbelieving mind. There she was, snack in hand, people jumping from the towers, smoke rising from the ashes, and she could have prevented…could have saved…could have helped…

Then, madness descended upon her.

Madness that caused her to thrash her beloved possessions in an uncontrolled dance of blind fury and finally, to collapse unconscious on her floor, collapse into a coma.

All was unleashed now, guilt over her dead friends and co-workers, endless rage over her uncle's cryptic email, anger over the vile attack on her city. All the demons that everyone around her spent weeks conquering—plus her own special demons courtesy of this uncle of hers—all this came out in an endless torrent.

Until there was no more, no more tears to shed, no more names to scream, no more anger to…

Spent.

A long time passed. Seconds, minutes, and hours seemed to merge with each other. Time was not measured the regular way; it was measured in units of pain, not in units of time.

Finally, Jenna reconnected, picking up the shards of her former reality, of her former self. All the weeks she spent pondering and feeling the agony of not knowing became distant memory. In only a few seconds, these memories seemed to fade away… She wished for it to reverse course to cover herself again with the protective cover of uncertainty…of not knowing, a sweet blanket of denial, of ignorance…of…

She raised her tearful eyes. She was lying in the hammock now, not quite remembering how she got there. Her tearful eyes were focusing slowly on her tormentor.

He was standing there. How could she not hate him? How could she not love him? How did he know? Why did he tell her? Why no one else? It couldn't be, it just couldn't!!!

All was screamed endless times, yet still these questions echoed in her mind. But now she was coherent again for the simple reason that all her energy was completely drained. It was like she couldn't move, not an eyelid, not a muscle, not a finger. Yet, in a small corner of her severely bruised mind, power was gathering.

Josh looked at her. He knew that the pain, anger, frustration, and guilt were still there. But he also knew that this was Jenna and that she wanted answers. He knew she was capable and competent. He knew that she passed this, the first of many tests to come. He had no doubts. His were good teachers. Nevertheless, a good omen is indeed a good omen.

It was no small feat, he reminded himself, to observe how his feisty red-haired niece hadn't let these emotions control her. Not even after she let everything out like that. "Are you ready for some answers?"

She nodded weakly.

"Let's take a walk," he said.

"A walk?"

"A walk."

They were seated at a false façade, somewhere in the West Village. It was an odd structure with a front wall and door decorating the sidewalk for no apparent reason and at the whim of city planners.

They were silently watching the crowds stroll by on a warm winter evening. "Why here?" she finally asked.

"I always liked places like this," said Josh, looking fondly at the mock front. "Ever since I was a young boy at the Museum of Natural History. Do you remember those elaborate displays? I used to look at those people from far-away tribes and I remember wanting to go inside the display. I wanted to be inside their reality, to merge into the distant horizon painted by skilled artisans, creating the feeling of vast distances, defying the small enclosure of the display. I always wanted to join in the happy hunting they were about to embark on, even though I knew that there was nothing there but cement wall behind the exhibit. Still, one could dream."

She shot a sideways glance at him. This was a bit out of character. She couldn't tell why. She would have probed further, but the evening and the drink were exerting their collaborative influence over her mind.

He kept going.

"Facades only—no depth. No space behind the decorative wall. We always like to think that when we go through a door, it leads somewhere. We like to think we know where it leads, yet here you can imagine that there may be something else, something not immediately visible. I do relish that feeling."

She smiled. She did enjoy his slightly archaic speech, his Uncle Josh speech.

He offered her the flask and she took another sip. All is as it should be. This time, the split-second imagery change was even faster than before.

"Come," he said, getting up and offering her a hand.

"Where are we going now?" she asked as she took his hand.

It was familiar pressure, easier to gauge and activate once the main link had been established.

"To the other side, Little One."

Jenna felt his fingers, felt turbulence in her veins. She felt that things were being erased from her vision as she crossed the door-less opening. A fog formed in her mind.

"The drink. It must have been the drink. The fingers, it must have been the fingers."

Her last conscious thought.

And since some (walked) in the way of righteousness while others walked in their transgression, the twelve disciples were called.

From the Gospel of Judas Iscariot

Chapter 7
"30"

"I am sitting here, staring at this bag of silver. With every fiber in my body, I want to take this Satan's offering and hurl it at the face of his emissary, run into the night, into the empty streets of Jerusalem, find my master and beg his forgiveness, be accepted back into the fold of my brethren and convince myself and convince them that the last days and weeks were all nothing but a bad dream.

Convince them that I am once more, the beloved disciple, the one who can be trusted, just like by the waters, at the storm, when the Roman troops surrounded us.

It is I, the one who has the power to defend my master and his disciples.

It is I, a rare breed amongst men of righteousness, amongst men of prayer, amongst men of sacrifice, amongst men of god. I, who stared at the jaws of death more times than I care to admit; I, who had the power to keep this holy group safe, nurture them in the bosom of our beloved Judea and away from prying Roman eyes.

It was I, with my trusted blade, the best Damascus steel, separating between the pursuing soldiers and their flame of life. Oh, my esteemed father would be proud of his son, carrying on in the Sikariki tradition, the Maccabi tradition. Our blades take life from our foes and give them to our brothers, to our comrades, to my master...and then...

When we felt one with our creator in the fields, on the march, in the dead of night when we were alerted that the legionnaires are looking for us, I was always the trusted, the beloved, and not just by my master but also by his beloved...

But no!

No!

No!

I know this is right, this is my lot to carry. It is my destiny to suffer through, cursed through the ages, how I wish I didn't!!! How I long not to be chosen for this dark task, but there is no escape, I am the only one! I know what needs to be done, I have been shown by the Lord's angel, the vision was thrust upon me, I have seen what will happen if I don't...accept this burden. And the silver—I have to accept that too. The legionnaires are much too cunning and will suspect if I don't.

I am here looking at the smiling soldier, his gleaming sword and spear, Longinus is his name and he is here to accompany me to make sure that all is carried out. And I am choked in internal misery, silenced by the immense truth that I have witnessed. The burden of centuries to come is here, now, on my tired shoulders. Even though the nails will not enter my flesh—I am the one who will be crucified, again and again from now to the world's end!

The angel's power flowing through my blind eyes, I could see the evil empire, the Roman hold on men. Body, soul and spirit all broken—I have seen, I have been shown by the divine powers how complete it is, how magnificent and how hopeless it is.

I have seen that if it continued to reign unchecked, if this evil hold on all that is human in us, on all that is godly in us will go on.

It will destroy our race to the point of no return. It will cover the world in darkness and all mankind will be thrown in the abyss, with no future, no hope, no salvation. And then, just as I was MADE to believe it all, just as I was able to grasp this...this truth, just then...

I was made to see that the one thing left to do was to show to the world that there was at least one soul that could not be conquered by Babylon. Even in death, the Romans could not humble and enslave this one soul, and that the world will see and hear and believe that if one soul could escape, then all souls could escape and that no matter how complete this Roman oppression is, there is still a way to defeat it. Yes! I have been shown that!

And yet, not to hear my master's voice again, not to bask in the glory of our companionship, not to share the spirit of our brave friends in our beloved sanctuary, not to defend him yet again with my trusted dagger. Not to return to a hidden, blissful shelter, eyes glittering in the night, tired and satisfied after another successful sally, another great sermon, another uplifting experience as we raise the oppressed, as we plant hope in desperate hearts and minds.

My brothers, my comrades, my master and his trusted beloved, all look up to me, all know that Judas is the one you can trust. The irony, the pain—Judas, from the trusted, the pillar of our fellowship. I will become the very essence of betrayal; mine will be the name men will evoke in hate, in fear, in anger, in the will of revenge. No one on this earth will know the truth, save these...these beings. I am told that in time, perhaps, wrongs will be righted, but I know that I will not live to see my name being cleansed; I am...

I am... I am...

It is of no use, Judas. It must be done; he has his cross to bear and so do I, to the end of time.

I can find some solace in knowing that his pain will end, while mine will linger. Come, Judas, the world is watching, Longinus and Pilate are waiting.

The Sanhedrin is gathering.

It must be done."

"As good and true men, they obeyed the king and carried out his commands."

Anonymous chronicler on the battle of the horns of Hattin. The battle that sealed the fate of the crusader's state in the holy land.

"A king does not kill a king."

Saladin, after the battle of Hattin

"Horns"

"Oh, what a cruel twist of fate! What an unimaginable turn of events. It is I, Raymond, who slew his first Saracen before I could mount a horse. It is I, who completed the perilous sea voyage from Outremer to the Christian lands more times than anyone in our squadron. It is I, Reymond, who spent countless hours with Chroniclers and bards, telling them of our deeds here, at the end of the earth.

It is I, who had the ears of the grand master, of noble Balian, of the father Patriarch—of the king himself, his sister, and now this new one, this usurper who is just weak enough so this unholy mission, this evil task that every fiber in my god-fearing body resists, this…shame…must be carried out.

And yes, I cannot deny it. Deep in my heart of hearts, I know that evil has seized us, that corruption had taken over, that we no longer fight for light, for truth, for god, for faith, and for Christian salvation. It is every man for himself; it is for wealth, for land. It is here are the unfortunate, the landless, the lawless, those who are born out of wedlock.

Product of the misplaced lust of their noble predecessors with common women, with whores and peasant wives, with Saracen seductresses and women of the high seas. Here they all come and fight. One day they are begging in the gutter, the other they are on horseback, commanding a raiding party against the caravan carrying silks and spices, gold and silver, on the road to Damascus, Aleppo, even Antioch itself!

It is true that we have to be stopped. I have known it even before I was approached by this…this…demon. No, not a demon, my simple mind cannot grasp the existence of this creature, yet I accepted it. I have traveled like Jeremiah, like Ezekiel…like Christ himself. I have been through the gates of heaven and hell, or so I was told…

I know, I can feel it in my whole being. And yet, my soul goes out to the thousands that will perish, to these regiments, splendid in their blues and turquoises, in their whites and blacks, the knights of the temple, my brethren, the knights of the hospital, formidable in battle. The king's own troops, surrounding the ultimate symbol of Christendom—the true cross.

The Flemish contingent with their colorful orange, the brave Germans, strange yet powerful…

…those we trained in our ways…all will be no more…come daybreak three days from today. I know they are in counsel. I know there are those who caution not to make haste, not to abandon reason in this folly.

Those who advise care are right; the lady of the lake will endure… Oh, I long to see the splendor of Tiberias once again. This lovely citadel, not the most powerful in Outremer, but the most joyful and beautiful. It is true that the master of the castle went seeking forbidden wisdom among the infidels. It is true that his messengers went far and wide in search of all the exotic trappings of the east, peacocks from India, soothsayers from Baghdad, scholars from Alexandria, draperies from the Higaz, countless amulets and drawings, jewels, and magnificent tapestries…presents from the Emirs.

The Padisah, the Sultans, the Caliph himself…

All this will burn, will be no more, and I am the one who will seal our fate.

I am the one who will set these lands ablaze.

I can't even take solace in my own demise. I have to see it through. After it is over, after Saladin's forces burn us like trapped animals, I will survive. I will carry out my destiny for the kingdom must linger. I have been shown what needs to be carried out. I will linger with the knowledge, with the horror, with the shame…

Knowledge that the cross must retreat for the sake of our human destiny.

Long have we raped and mutilated this country. The time of reckoning has come. Knowledge that in generations to come, wrongs may be righted. Would it be up to me and to those who will come after me, those who are listening to me…now? Is it the now? Can I hear them? Can they hear me? Alas, my mind cannot grasp this. Let me concentrate on my shame; at least here, in the burning guilt of my once proud Christian soul, I know what feelings assail me. I can understand them; I can be overcome by…shame, horror.

This great army of Jerusalem, this magnificent assembly of barons and knights, of foot soldiers and archers, of light cavalry and porters, all gathered to meet Saladin in one decisive battle, spoiling for war, for victory. For glory—all will be destroyed in not three days from now, all because the king is weak…and I have his ear. I will blind him to the dangers of the sun—baked road, to the Saracen field-burning arrows, to the scarcity of water in this harsh land. I will fill his eyes and ears and heart and mind and soul with the roar of battle, with the glory of the charging line, to save Tiberias, to save the lady, to save the kingdom…

I have done that before and will do that one last time…

For the sake of mankind to fulfill what I have seen…

Not a day ride from here, from the fragrant fields of Tzipori, from its springs and orchards, to the horn of Hattin, we will ride, we will fight, and we will die.

How I wish it wasn't I who was taken beyond the limits of my world, beyond the limits of my sanity.

How I wish it wasn't I.

It is my gift and my curse to you who will follow. May your lot be better than mine.

It is time; the king's council starts in an hour; I will whisper sweet poison in his poised ears, and we will be no more.

A cablegram was sent yesterday to Nathan Straus, who is in Rome, breaking the news to him that Isidor Straus and Mrs. Straus are among the missing from the Titanic disaster. Mr. Straus, who is not in robust health, was deeply affected. He has cabled for full details. Jesse Straus, son of Isidor Straus, with his wife and daughter, are passengers on the incoming Hamburg—American liner America. It is believed that they have not yet learned of the fate that has probably overtaken Mr. and Mrs. Isidor Straus.

The New York Times,
Thursday, April 18, 1912

"Legacy"

"I know that my words will be stored here. I don't fully understand the manner in which it will happen. I am afraid that I am out of my depth in these matters. Funny thing—it seems that running an international retail empire, developing the land of my ancestors, revolutionizing food consumption for an entire nation—all those accomplishments I used to take enormous pride in, all these marvelous achievements, all pale in comparison with what I now know, what I fully comprehend.

Yet—I cannot even comprehend the manner of which these words, these thoughts of mine will be stored. I have been told by my—for the lack of better word, let's call them my—guardian angels, that you, whoever may follow my footsteps, will be able to hear me. And yes, I now can hear the others as well, those who preceded me. I now can look back at this long line; I now know that this knowledge of my ancestry was blissfully kept away from me until the time was right.

All this knowledge, all this understanding, all this…shall we call it reconciliation? All this does not take one iota of the pain away, of the guilt away. Never did I fully experienced this, damned if you do, damned if you don't…

I was guided by the hands of my guardians, by the hands of my ancestors, and yet I thought I knew better. I thought I had it figured out. Alas, I didn't, and this is what I am trying to communicate to you, my unfortunate re-incarnation. Know this— yours will be an unhappy existence, compounded by other unhappy existences, sweetened only by the knowledge of this better cause, of this larger purpose. Even I, who ultimately failed my destiny, can help in some small way. For you can look at me through the hourglass of time and know what I did, know what I didn't do. And may it be of help to you when your time comes. At least, my words will help serve the purpose.

And what is this purpose you ask?

I will leave that to my angels, trapped in their icy castle, in their crystal palace, in their wondrous fiery cavern, to answer. They can do a far better job than I could ever dream of.

All I can do is tell you how this purpose was proven to me, proven beyond all doubt by this...this messenger that came to me that day in Palestine, as I was getting ready to reconcile with my sweet and impatient brother. I was getting ready to go back home, to let my community back stateside in on what needed to be done here in this 20th century, brand new, and struggling Palestine.

I was finishing everything when this previously unknown man appeared as if from nowhere, telling me that he was sent from Jerusalem, that I must go there, that the need is dire. And I went. I told my brother that he shall have to travel home without me. I went, even though secretly, I was looking forward to a bit of luxury, for a first-class meal, for French Champagne...

But I was convinced to stay, convinced by this man I have never seen before who held this...power, this...sway over me.

I should have known that the very fact that he was able to touch my soul with his words was suspect that something big was at play here. Something was amiss. I didn't; I didn't and the fact that I didn't is further testament to the awesome power of my angels of fire and ice.

I didn't suspect a thing.

I now know why.

And then, after I arrived, the world collapsed.

This invincible creature of the sea, this magnificent creation, this...TITANIC...it sank and took my world with it. Poor Isidor, poor Ida.

I was spared, but they were gone.

And then, in my deep misery, in my darkest hour, HE appeared again. He who saved my life. I was thanking him. Ha! The irony! If I knew then what I know now, I should have run far, far away, run for dear life.

But I didn't, and he had me hook, line, and sinker.

After all, I couldn't doubt him anymore, not after he had proven to me that he could tell the future. After all, what better way of doing that than to hand a man his own life as proof?

Or is it?

81

Perhaps it is I who is at fault, who was at fault...

What I am saying is, of course, it was I. In my hubris, in my pride, I thought I knew better and although the world keeps turning, I now fear greatly. For the news out of Europe, out of Germany, out of the land of Beethoven and Goethe, of Brahms and Wagner, is not good. And my heart is filled with misgivings, with apprehension.

He brought me here, where I will be ending this existence, where I know my former self will once again become a part of my next self. Where I am told to make this, this RECORDING, for you. Whoever you may be.

You see—I am Nathan Straus, millionaire, philanthropist, owner of Macy's, founder of countless charities.

I am Nathan Straus, inventor of safe food practice, of revolutionary food safety procedures.

But...

I am also a Watcher, albeit a failed one.

I am still part of this group; this tradition, this...lineage.

This...brotherhood who harbors our future. You can say we are cursed. You can say we are blessed. Cursed—because we really, truly KNOW, because we have to live with the consequences of actions so horrible that society's most hideous criminals will think twice before committing. Blessed, because we hold in our hand the faith of mankind and you may not believe me, but there is some solace in that.

It is I, Nathan Straus who escaped the Titanic as proof of my allegiance.

It is I, Nathan Straus, who helped Palestine overcome its first fragile phase of modern existence.

But...

It is also I, Nathan Straus, who was supposed to make sure that certain medical practices would become the law of the land in the western world just a few years later than previously estimated and as a result, a young German soldier would die from disease in the war to end all wars—the irony!

You see, I didn't perform my task. I thought I knew better; my pride, my arrogance blinded me...

And now...

This soldier is well on his way to lead his country. And although I will not live in this incarnation long enough to see the evil fruit of my decision blossom, I already have a heavy heart, for I know and hear things. Information does travel to me and I am afraid of what I have done or have not done.

Know that I will come back to consciousness. I will own up to what I have done, as horrible as it may be, why? Because on that spring day, I was shown the truth. I was shown that between the human race and oblivion, there is only a thin layer of defense; angels, men, and women. I was shown that the abyss is just waiting to open up and swallow all that is good in us, and that sometimes you have to commit evil to combat evil, and even though I was shown all that, at the time of action, I flinched. And I am afraid of the consequences. I will remain here. And my fear, my guilt, my shame will, in some small way, further the cause of my masters, my guardians, my friends and those to come after me.

Agartha, it is said, was not always underground and will not always remain there. A time will come, according to the writings of M. Ossendowski, when those who live in the communities of Agartha will leave their caverns and return to the surface. Once, before their disappearance from the visible world, they had another name but after their departure they took the name Agartha, meaning 'unreachable' or 'inaccessible', 'inviolable', because they found it convenient to establish their habitation of peace, according to M. Ossendowski, underground more than six thousand years ago. As it happens this dating corresponds to the beginning of the Kali-Yuga, or 'Dark Time' (the Iron Age) of western culture. Kali-Yuga is the last of four periods in which the Manvantara are seen. Their reappearance will be in harmony with the general purpose of the age.

René Guenon

Chapter 8

This time, the voice inside her head rang familiar, entangled in the dream sensation, yet not in the same way as those other voices. Those other voices were telling their own stories, whether or not there was an audience seemed irrelevant. They were almost like audio installations, sending their message in blind confidence to a blind universe. Secured in their own existence…looped.

But not this voice, this voice was different. Was it?

Addressing her? She started to listen.

"That's OK, Jenna, you can come back now. The others have come and gone, you can come back now, Jenna. The others are no longer here; it is OK, Jenna…"

As the voice receded to the background of her dreaming consciousness, Jenna was idly wondering about the odd choice of words. I am dreaming, her mind told her, so if I am dreaming, why does the voice say, "Come back, Jenna," and not, "Wake up, Jenna." Why does it sound familiar, but I can't place it, just like those dreams when simple tasks such as opening a door or turning the car key become impossible?

I had plenty of those dreams. I remember well. I was looking up a name on a list and the letters were blurring in front of my eyes. I was carrying groceries home and the bag kept ripping, counting change and all of a sudden, the coins became different…trying to close a door to no avail, to open one without success, so many times. Is this one of those times?

Is it one of those dreams where you can't move and you wake up to feel you actually CAN'T move? Or is it not a dream at all?

Am I dreaming now or is that a more complex form of the unsuccessful task completion dream? Is my dream task to figure out whether I am dreaming or not? It may be… But it doesn't feel like that.

It doesn't.

It feels like

like…

eyes opening.

Really opening.

Reality rushes in. Face looking down.

Familiar face.

Uncle Josh.

It is his voice.

But lips are not moving—what the?

His voice inside her head—Come back Jenna, the others are gone. Inside her head!!!

"What the hell?" escaped her lips as she jerked away from his gaze; an immediate vertigo followed, and she collapsed on the soft mattress.

His hand steadied her. It was becoming a habit.

Managing to control her breathing, Jenna looked up; the voice stopped.

This time lips were moving.

"Relax, Jenna," said Josh. "Damn that calm," she screamed inside her head. Mustering all her strength, she rose, supported by her elbow.

"Did you drug me, Uncle?" she asked. "I didn't know you were into that, and that voice, did you hypnotize me? Playing games, did you think this could do anything to make me forget?"

Her voice stopped abruptly. She focused on the horrible pain that permeated her universe since the discovery in his apartment. All that anger…wasn't really there!

She fully expected that with the return of her energy, there would be an immediate return of the fury, guilt, and pain.

But.

No—it wasn't like that at all—how could that be?

She could *sort* of feel the way she *used* to feel, but it was as if someone else were burdened with all that guilt and terror, fury, and anguish.

It was as if far, far away someone else was weeping for all those innocent lives lost, someone else was screaming in endless fury, someone else was experiencing all these terrible memories. It was someone else that was watching again and again as people were jumping out the windows, being incinerated in blocked

86

hallways and charred offices, clinging to life as walls collapsed, screaming in horror as flames licked flesh from bone, watching, again and again and again.

And again…

But it was someone else watching, far away. Not her.

Someone else and only a faint echo reached her consciousness…

"Why?" She started and changed her mind. Her uncle nodded thoughtfully when he saw the focus change in the green eyes of his beloved niece.

"I see," she said, a faint smile finally crossing her lips.

"Think about it as Advil for the mind," said Josh,

"Is that why I am not trying to rip your eyes out for what you did to me, what you did to all of them?"

He smiled, "Just a mild emotional pain killer. You have been through a lot and there is a lot more to come."

Completing her thought, "I see I have to make some changes in my perception of you," she said. "Either I am dreaming again or…or this is no drug."

"No drug," he agreed.

"And you are not just my sweet, eccentric Uncle Josh."

"No, I am not."

Jenna took it in. In her universe, everything was always organized, WAS always organized; she had to remind herself. Task and reward, work and play, mom and dad, Chris and Stephanie, uptown and downtown. Even her sallies out of her happy New York reality were always organized. Hell, even the magazines haphazardly spread over the coffee table were very carefully organized in their apparent chaos. All this was to no avail now as Jenna started to realize that this wasn't the end of the interruption into her Jenna-self but only the very, very beginning.

Fury set in.

"So what the hell is going on?" she erupted; even before she finished the sentence, she regretted it. Reality or not, it's not like her to snap like this, desperately trying to maintain composure.

Recoiling, collecting, careful. *That's* her.

"And that mental Advil of yours, is it meant to make me understand? Is it meant to make me not call 911? Or run like hell? Or pass out?"

She smiled then, her smile softening her words, taking a bit of the sting out. After all, it's her uncle. That much she still…knows, she kept telling herself.

"All the above and more," he smiled back.

"Well, there will pretty much have to be more to it than that now, won't it?" "I am glad you realize that," said Josh.

"And after it wears off? What then, will I again…?"

Hands on her shoulder, "So many questions, how about some more answers, Little One?"

She smiled again, the old Jenna smile, the one he knew from when he was bouncing her on his knees, from when the most challenging decision was what game to play or what books to read together. Jenna and Uncle, alternating who is the narrator and who is the audience. It was their favorite game.

But no, not now; now is not the time to indulge in long lost almost—innocence. "Come," he said and motioned her to join him.

"Aren't you going to give me some answers?"

"Better to show you."

For the first time since she woke up or whatever to call that state she was in, Jenna looked around. It was a small room, pleasing pale pastels, a chair, a table, a bed, and a door. "Where are we and where are we going?" she asked.

"To the inside."

"Inside?"

"Come," he said, "all will be answered."

Jenna didn't quite know what to expect as they stepped through the white door. Her most recent experience put a sharp divide between this universe and the one she once knew. A sharp divide between the last few hours and the decades that preceded them.

Somewhere in her mind, she knew that the mental sedative Josh had applied to her tired and aching mind, a marvelous riddle on its own, was keeping her from ripping the inside of her skull with fangs of anger, pain and doubt, from sinking into blubbering insanity. But what was beyond this step? What awaited her in this…unreal…reality? The bed and wall, and table and door, all looked so real, so nondescript, like a Motel 6 or a Comfort Inn room, almost ridiculous in their everyday feel. They were unreal because they felt so mundane; so real.

"Well, Alice," she silently whispered inside her head, "I hope it is real and I hope there is no rabbit hole beyond this door."

"And if there is, I hope it leads somewhere a bit more meaningful than a Mad Hatter tea party."

She decided that the room should be real. For a lack of a better option, it seemed real enough, but it couldn't be, or could it? "I guess it is zero hour, time to find out," she was thinking, grateful for the way her uncle was allowing the slow pace of action to mirror the deliberate pace of thought.

So what now? What is beyond this door? She couldn't see as she was stepping. It was all dark.

Really dark.

So, what now?

Alice?

Crazy images? A storm of emotions engulfing her senses? Time travel? Monsters and angels fighting their eternal fight?

Waking up on a cold floor? Ejected to a god-forsaken and abandoned piece of lane trapped between the roaring traffic of the New Jersey Turnpike as in this movie; what was it again? Was she being John Malkovich?

Or simply just waking up; all being one long dream, waking up to September 10th, waking up in her own bed, in her own apartment, in her own reality, in her own world.

She knew though…

She knew it was…

None of the above.

As they were passing through the door, it was actually…

It was…

Nothing

Absolutely nothing.

No sensation at all.

Everything erased.

Blackness, well not even blackness, more like no color, no sound, no feeling.

She tried to feel her own arm but couldn't; she tried to feel her own face but couldn't. She tried to feel her own weight but couldn't. It wasn't a sensory deprivation, tank-type sensation though. She couldn't feel—neither the movement nor the moved.

It was as if she was reduced to MIND only, THOUGHT only, all physical dimensions gone; is that what it feels like to be…dead? Was she? Was all that just a prelude to death? Was she still in a coma, on a bed in a hospital and all this was just preparing her? Could it be?

No bright light at the end of a tunnel? No heavenly music? Just being reduced to this…this…this non-self? What was it that she read a long time ago? What was his name? Gurdjieff? Was he the one talking about the mind becoming a mineral after death? Was that it? Was she turning into a mineral? Was that what being a crystal feels like? Was she turning into one?

But no, her thought told her no. "You are not dead, Jenna, you are still here. This is not death, too much left to do, too many questions left unanswered."

"What an old thought," played itself on her mind's screen. That's what old people think.

"Was I becoming old at some accelerated pace?" Maybe this was just another, more elaborate dream after all?

No.

Her thoughts told her that this was real; her mind told her that this was real.

And then, her mind, her thoughts, seemed to be getting smaller, smaller, fading into nothingness.

Everything kept fading. Fading…

So small that it seemed that she couldn't feel her thoughts. Much in the same way she couldn't feel her body just seconds ago. Only a small nucleus of awareness remained.

And it was getting smaller, sliding from the macro to the micro to the nano to the mezzo to the quark and beyond.
Smaller,
softer,
quieter.

Into nothingness, blissful nothingness, engines gracefully emitting a last burst in a sigh of unimaginable relief.

Full stop.

And then…

All of a sudden, a rush!!! A RUSH!!! A giant wave of…of…of EVERYTHING!

Every possible sensation assailed her newfound consciousness!!!

It was as if she was the sole representative of the human race, conceived and awakened to painful awareness upon the first sperm penetrating the first egg; down the eons of time immemorial. Evolutionary pregnancy at a frightening pace, experiencing all that humans experienced from before time began to where time is no more, all condensed and launched into one single germ of self, at Jenna.

Giant galaxies and subatomic particles danced in her mind's eye with an immense sensation of vast distances and the claustrophobia inside a single atom of hydrogen... Arctic chill mingled with a blaze of burning sun, thrusts of joy, fear, sadness, happiness, sensuality, and disgust. Her taste buds woke up, transmitting all flavors in a cacophony of sweet, sour, bitter, hot, and bland. All was raging in what seemed to be an eternity.

Or was it a nanosecond? She couldn't really tell. It was as if time itself were somehow suspended, somehow the passage, the most natural and automatic sensation, stopped from happening in this...this state, in...

That hurricane of brain cells firing on all synapses...

In some corner of her mind, she found a way to appreciate this, to remember that research had shown time and again that humans only use a small portion of their brain cells. Is that what it's like to experience a turbo gear in my brain? She managed to sneak in a thought in this cacophony of sensations.

Brief sensations of wars, of festivals, of great discoveries and tremendous works of art, of music, of science, of sheer elation that comes with exploring nature and all its wonders, science is all its glory, exploration, discovery, sex in all forms and ways, priceless delicacies sought after, truffles, monkey brains, caviar, the elation of the first Champagne created. Was she tasting it all? Savoring it all? Experiencing it all?

Stillness mingled with extreme speed. She was experiencing what she could only describe as a mental whiplash...moving faster than light and not getting anywhere. Star clusters storming in front of her eyes as her senses started to go into overload...colors screamed in her ears, sounds painted the insides of her eyelids in impossible shapes...tastes and smells were evoking emotions of joy...of fear...of...UNKNOWN; memories, her memories? Other people's memories?

Images of places and people, did she know them? Did she experience that, and THIS?

That and the other? She didn't know! She couldn't tell!

All she could do was to resist the weight of the assault.

Her mind started to dissolve. Her grip on who she was, on WHAT she was, started to slip away…away…into nothing… away…back into an isolated germ of awareness…

And beyond.

It seemed that everything was rushing away from her. Everything was getting further and further, smaller and smaller, faster and faster. Soon all became a distant sphere.

Then a small Circle.

Then a large dot. Then…

Gone. All gone.

And then, a voice spoke, and its speech was powerful, commanding, silencing all, resonating in her inner ear, much like her uncle's voice from…God, was that only a few moments ago? It felt like it was eons ago.

Thankfully, she realized that her inner clock was moving again, that the feeling of time suspension had left, that the flow of time was restored, at least for now…

And the voice was speaking, restoring calm. Adding more and more ability to digest what had transpired. For that, she was grateful, without knowing why or to whom.

Words rang faintly familiar, then she recognized them. It was a passage from the Bible! Seriously? She was thinking, again able to guide her thoughts.

How cliché it is, of all things. Bible? Give me a fucking break.

But almost in spite herself, she tuned in.

Yes, it was a…

A passage she actually knew. In another lifetime, she could recall how fifteen-year-old Jenna came across that passage and was wondering what it would be like… The passage was familiar but did contain parts that seemed new to her.

As the words rang, her body started to function again, to come back from the nothingness it had disappeared into, to feel again, arms, legs, the feel of clothing on her skin, the reassuring rise and fall of her breathing chest, her hair cascading down her neck. The knowledge that her eyes were actually closed this entire time rushed back. It was strange; her eyes were closed, and she didn't even know it.

But then again, it was as if she were almost afraid to open her eyes, as if she were content to let the gentle play of light and shadow dancing on her eyelids linger. Her brain could not anticipate what she would actually SEE at the other end of this...this...even the word 'EXPERIENCE' seemed not to fit. She felt that, as long as her eyes were closed, she could somehow hang on to shards of her former self, of her former world, from before fantasy became reality, became fantasy, became reality...ad nauseam.

The sensation that drove her to finally open her eyes was trivial, almost comical. It was as if she were in a slow descending elevator, the feeling was so familiar.

She almost expected to hear a Muzak version of 'My Heart Will Go On' or 'The Greatest Love of All' softly playing in the background...

Her eyes opened.

Into a...

Eyes transmitting visual information, well, some visual information.

Not everything around her was really visible, but her mind, using some popular imagery memories from Verne's journey to the center of the earth, Escher drawings, Asimov, Arthur C Clark, a trip to the planetarium, suggested some comparisons.

What was visible was so mind-boggling that it took several seconds before she realized that she was standing on...

Nothing.

That should have terrified her, but the fear was immediately purged by the sensation of support, physical support that engulfed her body, allowing the slow descent, allowing breathing and allowing support, acting on her physical self in a similar way it acted on her mental self.

The mental and physical were becoming interchangeable, so it seemed in this absurd reality. The thought seemed to be coming from outside herself. She welcomed that thought; farfetched as it seemed, it calmed her.

Back to trying to make sense of this place, this state she found herself in.

Like a piece of rock flying through space and suddenly waking up to consciousness in orbit over an unfamiliar planet. What was it in Adams' book, a whale? Was it a flower vase?

Some much-needed humor was still emerging in this OTHER side her uncle brought her to.

As far as she could tell, she was descending like a snowflake, almost as if she had no body mass, almost as if she were flying over an immense surface. Was it an enormous crystal? Mountain of solid volcanic lava…was that molten ice? Flames? Was it an asteroid? Was it a sun? A moon? A star? Was it made out of some metallic material that resonated on the edge of the color spectrum and seemed to be resting on white? And gold? And turquoise? "Fire," jumped into her mind, dancing flames licking giant ice sculptures? She couldn't tell.

Jenna had many flying dreams. Some were more real than others. The more real they were, the more disappointed she was when she woke up and realized she couldn't after all fly. In a way, this was like a flying dream. Was this another one of those? Would she now, finally, wake up? For the first time since it all began, she found herself wishing it was not so. Wishing that the flying feeling was real, in spite of everything that it implied, her uncle, his email, 9/11. It just felt so good to…fly? To get some distance, some perspective. Reality seemed to support her feelings.

Good.

As far as she could tell, she was gliding above this fantastic landscape, surrounded by darkness. Just as one would feel if one were able to fly over earth, in outer space, forgetting for a moment trivial things like mass, gravity, atmosphere. After all, she had already been made to forget so many things that defined her former reality. What were a few more?

She wished for a second that it WAS earth. That she would be looking at the blues and whites and familiar continent lines. But it wasn't like that. This felt a lot closer. It felt like dozens of miles, not thousands. And there was something else. She wasn't really flying. She was just standing there, almost like a straphanger in a subway car, descending through familiar darkness, her darkness.

More than just darkness, the darkness was transmitting, communicating, supporting. It even looked different, felt different. And when she reached out her hand, she could feel the texture of what was all around her, like moving through a cloud. No, not a cloud; her own coil of protective darkness.

Words escaped her, but she somehow knew that this medium she was moving through was used to communicate with her. She knew that the sensation of calm she felt was a postlude to the emotional hurricane she had just experienced and that the darkness had an important part to play. She was finding out bit by bit.

She was watching the vast surface from above, from her descending, friendly, dark coil, not that words like above or below had much meaning here. At times, it felt like she was actually rising and that her target was *above* her.

Looking around her, she could now glimpse other faint formations in the vast space that surrounded her. She wasn't the only snowflake in this immense…sphere? Perhaps sphere wasn't the right word.

Eyes and senses resolved their contrast and she was again looking at the spectacle unfolding under/over her, waiting for more details to emerge.

Her suspended sense of reality was accommodating; that much could be said. Jenna, that she was, adaptable on top of inquisitive, on top of ever curious, coming from a long line of Pandora ancestors. Reality, for now, didn't really count. This much she knew.

She accepted that in a Jenna-like practical sense. What was going to announce itself next? Did Alice actually reach the bottom of the rabbit hole? Suddenly, she couldn't remember.

Well, who knew? She knew that somewhere in her veiled self, unbelievable anger was still simmering, but the lid was on, for now.

All that intense thinking blazed in her head as the descent continued. It occurred to her that perhaps this timeout was given to her for precisely that purpose. Was that another outside thought?

Perhaps.

The soft, ethereal surroundings she was moving through shared the same quality with everything else she was looking at. It was as if everything was made out of everything. In a similar way to the sensation storm that assaulted her senses, the information transmitted to her five senses about the reality around her was made out of everything she ever FELT. It was like everything around her was made out of…well…faint glimpses of everything she could think of, metal, stone, cloth, shell. Wood, wool, other sensations, maybe this is what thought felt like when she touched it?

Maybe this was what it felt like to touch her soul? It was different from before. In some strange way, the uncertainty of WHAT she was moving through, of WHAT she was surrounded by, didn't seem to weigh heavily on her stretched sense of self. It almost had a calming effect.

Somewhere in Jenna's organized mind, this information was collected, collated, and stored for future use.

So, where was she? The mundane question kept returning.

Somehow, she felt like this whole place was somewhere underground or perhaps again, she was dreaming. She felt, as before, that this 'place' was immense, yet it also felt like it could be very small, like the sensation of vast distance and space that could be found in an illusion created by skilled painters?

Was she inside a painting? Was she inside a sculpture? Was she inside a jewel? Dreaming that she was inside a painting? Dreaming that she was inside a sculpture? Dreaming that she was inside a jewel? She remembered, smiling, the light dancing gently on the giant crown jewels as she went to glimpse them for a second time, all those years ago. The rapid pace of the moving belt surrounding those magnificent objects was moving at a pace that was too fast for young Jenna. She simply HAD to take a second look!

Descent was coming to an end as the surface materialized all around her.

She came to rest in a shallow cavern. All around her were fantastic colors and formations of all the shades and colors she saw in her flight. From here, they seemed no less spectacular. There was movement inside these walls that now surrounded her. She will be looking there soon…

Her eyes informed her of a more solid footing. Her legs didn't quiet agree. She was able to stand. She was able to…

Another snowflake was arriving. Uncle Josh, just in time.

Uncle's steadying hand guided her as she was slowly regaining her footing. "There," he said, and she saw that out of the forms inside the…the…

"We call it IceFire crystal," said Josh quietly, sensing her need. "It's not such a good name, but we came to accept it."

"We?"

"Not now."

Jenna felt a mental finger on her lips. Then she felt her mind opening up to the forms she half-saw inside the…IceFire. They were more like silhouettes but seemed to have depth. They were not steady. They kept changing their impression on her retina. She didn't know what she was looking at; were they faces? Eyes? Were they vortices of light?

Blazing stars? Flickering wings? Slow-motion electrical currents?

She couldn't tell.

But she did know that it was their voice that quoted the biblical passage before. And she knew that her newly found inner ear could listen to them. With that knowledge came the knowledge that they were about to speak again. She was composed enough, calm enough, and curious enough.

Or so it seemed.

"What you experienced for a short time when you entered here is what we experienced for times so vast they cannot be measured by human standards," said the voice inside her head. It was a comforting voice, pitched just between a man's and a woman's, carefully pronounced. Jenna briefly thought about Kenneth, the guy from her office whose origins no one knew, and his oh-so-carefully pronounced English. Smiling, she remembered, and then recalled that Kenneth was no more, burned to a crisp in the flaming…

"Not now," said Josh again. Jenna recoiled slightly, her mental sedative covering the painful memory.

Realizing that the OTHER voice was completely aware of her thoughts, she felt like she sneezed in the middle of a concert and could even feel herself blushing a bit.

"It is quite all right," said the voice and Jenna could feel waves of empathy and affection reaching out to her, and yes, a bit of amusement, of carefully veiled humor. It was odd to feel such a human sensation emanating from such a non-human…whatever-the-hell it was. Following suit was the 'Hey, I am not a puppy' knee-jerk reaction that was pure Jenna.

She stopped herself. After all, she was dealing here with something much bigger than herself, if this was indeed all real and not a product of some form of mental collapse, dream gone wild, drugs or all of the above. Mark your correct answer Jenna, or stop interrupting and let's resume regular scheduled programming, on with it…

"…vast amount of time," continued the voice. "When we were sent here, we were completely…unprepared for this MATTER of yours; we are energy creatures, swimming in the cosmic ocean. Flickering across time and space, not even that. Maybe non-time or non-space is a better description. The non-feeling you experienced for a short time is our natural condition. It is calm and it restores us. Yet we share with you the urge to venture beyond the natural state, the root of all things."

The voice paused. It was hard to believe, but as she was adapting to it; IceFire was adapting to her.

"You see, we have been communicating with humans since they first existed," said the beautiful voice, "and until recently, this would be our way of addressing your curiosity as to what we are. But now, with you, we can go further you see. What you experienced is all matter, for the division between matter and energy, substance and thought, is purely artificial. It was put in place to protect, to protect it from you, to protect you from it. Where we come from is the only place where matter, in any form, cannot penetrate, the only place where pure existence is allowed to exist. When we came here, we had to experience what you experienced, only on a much larger scale."

"Why are you telling me all this? Why did you have to take me through all this?" Jenna formed an immediate response, still Jenna, still the inquisitive mind, even now, even in this non-reality, she would stick to her guns.

"You need to know who we are, to experience who we are in order to find out who you are, to experience who you are." Was the voice getting a bit agitated?

"Well, that sounds like a Chinese fortune cookie and I hate Chinese food."

Jenna was thinking. She DID hate Chinese food, all this heavy spicing. You eat and eat and at the end, even though you feel bloated, you just don't feel full! The only thing she DID like about Chinese food was no mess aspect of it. How Stephanie puts it? "Food that comes in a bag and leaves in a bag," inner smile to her inner self.

Restraining hand on her arm, and Jenna knew she pushed a bit too far, recess over.

No fear, just a feeling of foot-in-mouth, and strangely, again the wave of affection from inside the thing, the IceFire crystal, was it? It may have been agitated. It may have welcomed the sensation.

"Joshua, you may have been right," said the voice and Jenna knew both of them heard it. She remained silent though, as Josh gestured to her to stay quiet.

"Then," said the voice, "time started, matter started, and our one, the one who *exists* made us aware of what was to be, of a universe being created to fulfill a destiny yet unrevealed. With solid time and solid matter came a desire to disrupt solid time, to disrupt solid matter. We fought this, this distortion, which fled to the world of matter; the one could not follow into the matter dimension, to what the matter dimension had become.

As matter was getting too thick to penetrate, too dense with life to engage without destroying what was already in progress. You see, we existed in the purest matter-thought and matter-time form. The struggle created other matter, thicker and thicker, cruder and cruder, until a decision had to be made and we…

We were chosen to come here, to descend into this world of crude matter and guard it against the distortion that became what you know as evil. Again, matter, as you call it, is beyond what you call it. Matter can be made from all that exists. From metal and wood, but also from thoughts and dreams, urges and feelings, desires and sensations, and many, many more possibilities that are hard to put to words in your pedestrian way of communication. Evil found its way into matter and temptation grew, evil grew. And we were sent here to counter that effect, to bring a pure source of matter to the world that was being corrupted."

What she could feel was not satisfying; perhaps there was a way to make sense of all that matter stuff, even make sense of the way IceFire was apparently repeating itself. Some of what she was hearing was hovering on the edge of logic.

The rest would have to wait.

She tuned back in.

"…we defeated it, but in defeat, we were defeated as well, for we were infected with desire, and with matter and with this world."

Jenna knew then why she heard what she heard. Words started to solidify into a cohesive feeling of connection. Suddenly so trivial and primal, it made her want to laugh and point, and she was thankful for her uncle's mental medication.

Somehow, she felt that any number of comments she may have to this story would not be appreciated, forgetting that this voice already knew what she wanted to say before she said it. She couldn't help it though. "It was so easy for men to get laid in ancient times; all they had to do is to say, 'I came from God baby, let's get it on,'" escaped her desperate attempts to control herself. Damn! Her BRAIN was blushing.

"It is quite right," said the voice repeatedly, more than a little amused. "The one you call your uncle has made us aware of your…unique qualities and we welcome them, as you can see we have been here for a long…" The voice felt as if it was/they were actually smiling, and Jenna felt warmed by the sensation.

The scripture resonated in her head once more.

"The sons of God saw the daughters of men, that they were beautiful and comely, and they took wives for themselves of all whom they chose…"

"Yes," said the voice, "In a last act of desperation, evil has trapped us here. For after we became desire, we became flesh and we could no longer return to our dimension." And Jenna could hear a faint sense of longing, more vast than she could ever imagine; what a burden! What a sense of loss, and all she could feel was a mere shadow of that vastness.

It reminded her of watching the last gasp of a giant 30-foot wave, when it reaches your feet at the shore. You can only imagine the force and splendor, the vastness and enormity of the wave out there in the open ocean. Its glory. Its majesty and awesome power and yet, it is here on the sloping sand, licking your toes in a gentle touch, evoking in you distant imagery of its faded grandeur, peacefully fading into nothingness on a soft bed of sand.

This is how she felt in the brief moment, as the nostalgic fog that emanated from IceFire passed through her, gently licking her mind's toes.

Her humorous, cynical mind couldn't produce anything to counter that effect. For once, she was left naked with a sincere emotion. Her mind bowed under that weight of such an emotion. Perhaps an inhuman weight of an emotion was needed here to get under her defenses, producing a human result; a Jenna result, as much as she was trying to deny it.

"For a while, we could move about your world. We could communicate with our offspring and theirs and with men and women of bright mind, for matter was new and still saturated with more delicate forms of matter, of thought matter, of energy matter, of dream matter. Matter was connected to what we were, to where we came from."

After a brief pause, as if to mark a transition, IceFire continued, "Faint echoes of those days are left in your people's tales of Gods and heroes, of magic and wonder, of the holy grail, the philosopher stone, of Gilgamesh and Krishna, of Hercules and Noah, Jason and Thor, of burning bushes and talking rocks of Isis and Osiris, Arthur and Merlin, Abraham and Malchizedek.

A flicker of memory was set loose—Osiris—what was that lecture she attended at the…what were they? Rosi something, oh yes, Rosicrucians, this crazy boyfriend of hers, something about the third eye, the eye of Osiris, the glands, the…"

Again, she was able to halt the flow. IceFire was waiting patiently and politely. Jenna felt as if a distinguished professor was allowing the promising young student an outburst of sorts. "…later," was mind-whispered to her from aside, Josh.

"But evil was always present. We tried to stem evil as best we could, for this was our only hope and mankind's as well. If we could help mankind evolve in the way we know our one had originally conceived, both mankind and we will finally be able to return to the cosmic non-space and non-time we so long for, you so long for."

"Evolve?"

"Matter," said IceFire, again the distinguished professor. IceFire was adapting to Jenna in much the same way she was adapting to…it?

"…has a way of evolving and devolving. In due course, you will know everything you need to know. For now, suffice it to say that matter evolves and devolves as a result of our actions, us, you, those who oppose us. Think about the world the way it was millennia ago, centuries ago. Think about the cruelty, the barbarism, the worthlessness of life, the casualness of death, the slow agonizing journey toward peace and understanding, toward order and stability." (Inquisition, Holocaust, MONGOLS, flashed in her mind) "All these developments were aided by us. If we can continue to guide, to nurture, to support and to assist, matter will evolve and so will we, and so will you."

"On the other hand…

If the enemies keep their action on course, the darkest episodes in your history will be but a mere prelude to what will transpire."

"And the only salvation lies in the path that is outlined from time immemorial," IceFire resumed its distant manner.

"Even if we don't know it," she was thinking.

"Even if you don't know it," the crystallized walls around her thought-echoed. "Again, traces and shades of all of this information are numerous in your tradition, in Avesta and Kabala, in Vedas and Surahs, in your medicine and alchemy, in your Hermatica and tarot cards, your Cain and Able imagery."

"In your time measurements and number system, in your art and music…seven days of the week…the seven-note octave, the octave itself. It was suggested and dismissed that higher octaves meant higher matter. It was suggested and dismissed for the timing was too early, astrological symbols…music of the spheres…some of it was of our choosing, some was not."

Jenna had to interject at that point.

"What if Stephanie was here," went through her head, briefly remembering all those friendly arguments about various conspiracy theories. "She would go crazy with joy." Her concern for her friend was resurfacing. "You better be right, Uncle," she was thinking. IceFire continued:

"As time progressed, so did the evolution of matter, and we found we could no longer take active part in the world. Men and women we tried to connect with could no longer hear or see us, and if we insisted, our matter—energy would burn too bright and they would die. Incinerated. Orpheus losing his wife to the dark lord of the underworld, Krishna shot by an arrow, Uzzah electrocuted by the ark-of-the-covenant, ascension of Elijha, of Hanoch…"

102

The voice was sad for a moment, lost in a private lament echoing over the millennia. "Long have we mourned for those who died, and finally, we realized that a change was needed and we retreated here. We willed this…location into existence for we can still summon power over crude matter, even if it comes at a great cost to us and requires a great deal of recovery. We created this place. This refuge."

"Funny thing," she was thinking. "A lot of what I am hearing is wide, popular knowledge; how come I never heard about…"

Intercepted and answered by the figurines trapped inside the mirrored crystals, "We knew that word of this sanctuary would leak out."

"It was inevitable as communication needed to be maintained. But we endeavored to stem the source as best we could. We were fairly successful as only a faint whisper found its way into the world's consciousness and only in recent times, Agartha under the mountain, was the name that was whispered for centuries. And even in that name, the truth is appropriately…veiled."

Again, that breath of the most human quality of them all, humor. Maybe that, more than anything else, made Jenna more than just a listener. Even if she did feel it was done on purpose, it was still effective, maintaining a link between her humanity and that of this overwhelming entity. Yet she remained skeptical. Jenna that she was, positive, optimistic, matter-of-fact, cynical, hyper-organized, ever endeavoring to overcome her physical impression on the world and make the world (fiery crystal was the world here) understand what a force she was, defensively and offensively.

Her defenses were not easily overcome. Being told what to do without fully comprehending the how, why, where, and when was never her strong suit. And there was more to come.

The voice paused. Not that it took a supernatural intelligence to crack the code of Jenna's face. After all, she was the first one of this brassy, technologically savvy, instant gratification, deeply suspicious of everything that came before it—to be brought here. "So you ran and hid? What kind of a superpower are you?"

"Why hide under the excuse of not wanting to hurt men? Why not use your powers to fight the enemy?" She couldn't help it. She knew she was being blunt, a bit crude, childish even.

However, even though she FELT the truth behind the words, she couldn't help it!

She knew that countless souls before her asked these very same questions. She knew that these cries echoed in ancient temples and hidden grottos, in sacred oak forests, by sweaty crazed sorcerers in Shamanistic caves, and in the splendor and elegance of Europe's courts. Some of the names flashed quickly in front of her eyes—Trithemius, St. Germain, Roger Bacon, Pythagoras, Ashmole, Helena Blavatsky, John Dee, Plato, Eliphas Levi... She knew that her thoughts were not original, that her anger was not new.

She was too smart not to know this, but here, now (if there was an actual HERE and NOW) facing this, this...THING, she couldn't help herself.

"Why whine about your enemy? Why not stand up for what you want and for what you believe in with conviction and fucking fight for it?" was written all over her consciousness, over her inner face.

IceFire, of course, knew all this. Hence the pause, letting the brightness of reason and logic have their way with the inevitable rage—so futile, so charmingly...human.

"Are you ready for your answer?"

She didn't have an honest answer for that particular question. "You see," IceFire radiated with seraphic patience.

"We knew that if we further interacted with this world, if we further contaminated our essence with its crude matter, its twisted desires, we would lose the thread that still connects us and the infinity from which we came. Yes, we were punished for doing it in the first place. But we were also left a window of hope. Entangling further in the matter world will close that window, to us and to you. There is no return if this window is closed."

Understanding.

Followed by comprehension.

"And the rules were written."

"She is a quick one." IceFire realized. "Too quick?"

"Still, we needed to guide and monitor, to help and nurture; we were, we are the Watchers over men, but we could no longer do it directly. We could no longer watch. Or perhaps it is better to say that we could no longer ACT as Watchers."

The voice went silent and Jenna felt the weight of the words; it made her realize how childish her previous rage over this seemingly immense injustice was. "How come the bad guys always have the biggest guns," how childish indeed, childish yet inevitable.

A new thought was entering her mind, could it be? Is she?

"You are starting to understand," the images inside IceFire were almost faces now. And as they were turning their almost eyes on her, she trembled a bit. It is one thing to get angry, another to realize what she was realizing.

"There are only half a dozen of us left," said the voice, now pitched in a beautiful unison effect. "In different traditions, the number is seven, as in the seven days of the week, notes of the musical scale, deadly sins, seven Rishis of the Hindu tradition…the seven Orisha of Nigerian and Caribbean voodoo…but that is because the evil, out there…was once considered one of us."

Jenna was looking at the glimpsing figurines that stretched out on this real/unreal plane. Many of them, but the inner light was shining from only a few. She knew, almost abruptly that the darkened structures were casualties, just like her own world had. Her sympathetic mind was reaching out, to the other side of awareness and was welcomed with…was it gratitude? Gratitude from a shiny rock?

"They passed away from longing," came the thought back, together with the gratitude and acknowledging Jenna's empathy. Longing. Like a pet waiting for his owner, like an angel longing for his/her God.

IceFire was unprepared for that. Allowing this young, impulsive, and impressive human under the crystal skin, a taste of its own medicine, a sensation long forgotten.

Jenna was indeed special. Futures flickered quickly, time for the present though.

"So we turned to the product of our original sin," said the beautiful voice, echoes of long forgotten memories.

"Each one of us has chosen six offspring to carry out the Watchers' mission. With great effort and in very specific ways, we can help on occasion. With a very strict set of skills and attributes, we can aid humanity on its journey upward. And we need you, the six need the 36; you are our human agency to help shape what is to be."

"Thirty-six," whispered Jenna, "Why is that number so familiar?"

"Lamed Vav," came from her side, her uncle was talking in his actual voice, with strange formality. "Lamed Vav," the Hebrew letters adding up to 36 in this math-characters method she sort of knew.

"Of course," she knew now, "The Lamed Vav, the 36 hidden righteous ones from Talmudic legend."

"Who would have thought?"

"As you can see," said IceFire's voice as Jenna started to call it, "There are clues out there, but never more than clues, for it is a delicate balance."

"Although it is good to have these faint echoes of truth ringing in the world, it is also extremely dangerous."

"Evil…wearing many guises is always out to destroy us, to find a way inside here, into our sanctuary. If this happens, there is no telling what that event will yield."

"So why…?" escaped her mind. Again, amusement from IceFire.

"You know the answer to that…Finding another layer and bringing smiles to both human participants…Little One."

"I swear I'm starting to dislike this nickname," said Jenna out loud, in a mocking/serious tone. What a sensation—making a rock laugh.

Jenna was pleased. Comic relief is always welcome in the middle of mind-boggling revelations. "What would all my dungeons-and-dragons friends give to be here and to hear all that?"

"…yes, you know the answer to that," continued IceFire, "clues are important for human evolution, for our evolution. We expend a lot of energy to combat the evil forces and you, the 36 are a part of that defense. You, the 36 have genetic markers that come directly from us; perfectly preserved throughout the millennia in your mitochondrial DNA. These markers will enable you to become who you were meant to be."

"They already had helped," went through her mind; the communication, the drink, the voices inside her head, the coma itself; understanding was gathering and taking hold. She couldn't help but muse on what would happen when this understanding would confront the rage she still knew simmered in her. Who would win the fight?

IceFire continued.

"In time, we will give you the forces and guidance needed to accomplish this part of your mission." Mission?

Nobody said nothing about no mission! Triple negative to triple voice her anger.

She didn't know she was being recruited; correction, of course, she knew, but a sense of self, of choice, announced its presence, together with a sense of "You got to be kidding," and "What the hell are you talking about?"

She will just let them fight it out.

Jenna felt that it was better that way. After all, there was a lot to digest before seeing herself in some superhuman, superhero existence.

Like a damn cartoon.

"...this place, our existence, and power need to stay hidden until the time is ready, and you, the Watchers' Watchers are how we can still combat evil and assist men. You help us out there and we help you in here."

With a sense of closure, the shades inside IceFire were subsiding, colors returning to the forefront of her vision.

Jenna felt unsatisfied. "Was that all?"

What about those strange people whose minds she seemed to have inhabited earlier; what about her pain? What about her coma? Her guilt? Her anger?

What about the falling towers? Questions remained...

She was once again moving. And IceFire was changing colors again, fading colors into the white mist of ice, away from the bluish-purple flames, disappearing into immeasurable distances, into its space-defying matter. A sense of loss engulfed her, completely unexpected. Beyond the unfinished quality of the moment, she felt like she was left at the platform, a train disappearing in the distance. Much left unsaid.

"Was that all? Why the sadness?" She should be angry, hurt, indignant, sarcastic, not sad! Hand on her elbow.

"I will supply the rest," said a voice next to her. Uncle Josh! She almost forgot he was there.

"I know there are more questions," he said, "I know how you feel." Did he?

"Answers met with more questions. I know that you need a bit of a break, some food, and some rest."

"Let me get it straight," said Jenna with a mouth full of vegetable stew, steamed to perfection by her uncle.

"You are…"

"I am."

"And you want me to…"

"I do."

"And those people that I felt are part of…"

"In a manner of speaking."

"It is a good thing, Uncle, that I am still under the influence of whatever you did to me." Then another thought announced itself…

"But," she said. "You're not my…don't tell me," she jerked away. "Are you?"

Josh smiled, "Oh Jenna, even The Six are now familiar with the temper and spunk of my darling niece. Of course not."

She believed him, a sigh of relief, thinking briefly about a darling father and his pipe, his paper, his 'Oh Shoshana'—her Hebrew name. "Then how come I am…here?"

"Genetics is a flexible concept when it comes to the Watchers," he said. Cryptic as it might sound, it did restore calm.

She smiled. "Hey that's not a way of getting out of giving me a straight answer about all of this now, is it?"

"No."

"So, the guy with the knife obsession, the one with the bag of coins, is he really who I think he is?"

"Yehuda, yes he is."

"That's great. Just great. The most hated person in history and I am a descendant."

Josh was visibly upset.

"No, Jenna, you need to understand! He did what he did because The Six showed him! They pointed the way! They were just! As was he! You have to stop thinking about him like that!"

"Showed him what?"

"What would have happened if Yeshua didn't die on the cross." "And what would that be?" Jenna fired back.

"Couldn't it just not be? Not happen in the first place?"

"All that blood and suffering?" Even to herself, she sounded a bit plaintive, but nevertheless, real.

Josh measured his response; this was a point of very crucial timing.

"If the cross didn't happen, the Roman hold on human life would go on unchecked, enslaving the world for many more decades, even centuries, leaving no hope to the oppressed, just a boot planted on their neck. So much time would have passed in that state that it would have taken a lot longer to start bringing the concept of freedom to the world. So much time would have passed that it may have been impossible to do that."

"Yeshua showed the world that a man could escape that tyranny; the world needed to see that. The seeds of Roman collapse in the 5th century were sown in Jerusalem. Better remember that, Little One, when you feel ashamed of your ancestor; you should be proud of him."

That silenced her. Could it be? Could such a pivotal event, such a historical turning point, such a...she was at a loss finding more ways to describe the enormity of this...could this be...planned?

Manipulated into being? Engineered into existence?

"That doesn't matter," she flared up, "He is still the most hated person there is! There ever was! His name is the very synonym of...and I am...!"

She couldn't quite finish the sentence and stopped for air.

"Indeed," said Josh. He and his damn indeeds. But he was right. She did hear those...those DEAD thoughts, and he was right, Damn him! The more Jenna knew she was wrong, the more it was difficult for her to admit it. She smiled weakly at him, and he knew that this particular lesson had sunk in, deep.

"This is what we do here with the Six. They have this power from their original dimension; they are still able to manipulate ours, all our dimensions, matter, time, and beyond matter and time."

"They are careful not to disrupt matter, external and internal, as they explained to you but time, what we call alternate dimensions, possible futures... They can see what would happen if certain things happen or do not happen and what the consequences would be and they show us."

"So you do their dirty work for them," Jenna said in a small, bitter voice.

"If you want to look at it this way, then yes, but this is for us as much as it is for them, Jenna; you have to remember that."

"Is that all? They show you simulations, hallucinations or whatever you want to call these tricks? That's it?"

Josh smiled; it was a memory smile. It was a good smile, she knew this one.

"You just thought about your young self, didn't you?"

He nodded thoughtfully

"Amazing, the similarities and the differences, truly amazing. And no, this is not all. There is power here, lots of it, power to combat what is wrong, to do what is right, all in good time. I do hope you believe me, Jenna."

She took time to contemplate that.

"I do believe you," she said, and she believed she did, at least for now. "And the others, what about the others?"

"The temple priest is the earliest of our line we can remember; before him it goes too far back."

"Too far back? What does that mean?"

"This is the hard part," says Josh, "Well, one of them."

She looked at him and smiled; can anything be more difficult than the mind-blowing, reality-shattering experience she just endured in the presence of these ancient voices? Not to mention three months in a coma, a cruel flood of guilt and fury, shame and anger...and a journey through some very strange and disturbing imagery right inside her mind? Not to mention the alternate reality she was just presented with. What can possibly be harder?

"I know," said Josh. "You think you have seen it all, but there is more, you see. I am indeed your Uncle Josh, but I am more than that. As you know we are descendants of the union between the original Watchers and humans; as such, we do not live a regular life span."

Jenna felt her mind blow open again, all these stories she loved to read. What else will happen here, Leprechauns? Dybbuk? Count Dracula? Elves? Count of Saint Germain?

He smiled; he saw her esoteric book collection a number of times.

"Well, I can't blame you for the look on your face. The truth is that as a part of the 36, we are, in effect, immortal. We exist until we…choose to stop existing."

This hit home. They both knew that if Jenna was in complete control of her faculties, all hell would have broken loose at the moment.

Given her sedated state, she remained silent. But being Jenna, in a remote corner of her mind, an almost thought was starting to form…an almost idea presented itself to her… She was hardly aware of it. "He is definitely unaware," her mind's eye was thinking.

"We can reincarnate multiple times, and I have been different people before I was Josh, your uncle. You see, we come here to rejuvenate and we go back into the world as a different person. We can choose to be born or to assume an identity of a grown individual. The Watchers can adjust timelines and create smooth transitions for us; it is part of their powers…"

Josh continued, in a musing tone.

"We do have the choice to be reborn and in maturity, receive those other memories that are stored here or to appear as adults. In different times, I have chosen both paths, but as the world becomes such an ORGANIZED place with borders, chips, passports, ID cards and digital life, I feel that appearing out of nowhere may not work all that well."

She desperately wanted to ask him the obvious question, "Were you…?"

She felt she had better not; perhaps it was IceFire's influence, perhaps not, or perhaps it was better not to know. Some things are better in shadow than in the harsh light of reality, of actuality. After all, she loved her uncle and she wanted him, at least in part, to stay her uncle, so she could keep loving him. An anchor against what was to come. Jenna desperately wanted to be able to hold on to untainted feelings and precious memories; would she be able to?

She thought she could. Moving on…

"All that is well and good," she said, "But aren't you forgetting some tiny detail, dear Uncle?"

"And that is?" Damn Jewish, answering a question with a question. Even under her mental sedative, she felt the remote waves of pain and anxiety. Concentrate, Jenna! Concentrate!

"Aren't you going to show me why all these people had to die? Why the towers had to fall?" "Why I was lying there in a coma with all these crazy voices ringing inside my head? Why I am carrying all this guilt now without anyone to share it with? Everyone will think I've completely lost my mind…"

And with that, memories of Stephanie, of Chris, of her parents, of her friends and co-workers flooded her for an instant, that and a sense of immense loneliness. It subsided though; something inside her fought all this, on its own. Perhaps it was a part of her new self.

She was letting this go and was back on the surface. Facing her uncle, her tormentor, her savior.

"What do you think, Jenna?" Question with a question.

She collected herself. Her tired mind recalled recent voices.

"If Judas was shown, why Christ had to be crucified, and he was convinced as I felt he was, then I guess I will be too, won't I?"

Skeptical Jenna, torn between the enormity of what she would have to endure to follow that simple logic and the feeling of resignation that still clung to her from this ancient voice echoing through the millennia.

"Here," said Josh, offering her the flask. She sipped. Her eyes were on him. "Remember I told you, later…"

"About Osiris, about the…the third eye."

He nodded; Jenna never ceased to amaze him. He was glad things were, so far, progressing well.

"Yes, precisely, about the third eye, that myth about people that are able to see into the spirit world. You will find out that many such myths are based on distant memories that are buried somewhere in the collective consciousness…"

"Third eye included?"

"Three for the price of two?"

"No extra charge?"

"Third eye included, and that is one of the simple ones to comprehend."

His smile was defying the gravity of this assertion, but she knew. She knew that there would be more to come. In her Alice-imagery, she desperately wanted to yell "BOOH!" and make all that had happened turn into a pack of cards and collapse into nothingness. She wanted her old self back; she wanted her old

112

world back. But she realized that the very thought of her world as old made it so. There was a brave new world to face.

Josh was patient. "May I continue?"

Her tired smile thanked him.

"You see," he resumed, "we have these two small glands inside us, the pineal and the pituitary glands. They are not quite part of the brain. They regulate the flow of…"

"I know," she says, "something about hormones: melatonin, right?"

"Yes, but with the potential to do much more than that. Long ago, even before my time, those glands were a lot more developed, and they were connected to matter and time and dimension in the ancient way. They were even visible to the naked eye, on the skin, protruding, like a third eye."

"Unicorn," escaped her lips.

His familiar smile flashed for a split second.

"Yes. Unicorn is a legend based on these forgotten memories. But we, the Watchers, still have capability to connect; it comes from our DNA."

"Then what about the flask?" She asked. "Is this drink like an amplifier of sorts?"

"Of sorts," he agreed.

"And more, but there is no time now. You said it yourself; you wanted to know, to be shown."

She nodded her agreement.

Josh repeated the ritual from before, fingers finding their delicate place. Jenna, almost subconsciously, stored the memory of his actions.

"You are ready," said Josh, "see for yourself."

Jenna watched how the West, hobbled by inertness and complacency, ultra-liberalism and twenty-four carat Western guilt, became a target for waves of fanaticism emanating from the East. She watched how the advancing waves of Islam, fifteen hundred years after their initial onslaught, finally adapted to fight the enemy on their own terms. How the Islamic version of democracy—one person, one vote, one time—proved more effective than bombs, tanks, and armies. Country after country voted in favor of Islamic rulers and those rulers transformed their victory into a Sharia victory, France, Austria, Hungary, Denmark, Eastern European countries…

She watched how, without the shock of 9/11, and under the guise of democracy, more and more countries ended up covering their women, crescents flying high, Christians and Jews oppressed, and finally religious fever sweeping across the Atlantic and into the last bastion of freedom as the stars and stripes gave way, as the USA became UISA, United Islamic States of America. All unfolded in front of her eyes in a quick jump-cut action sequence that, while fast and furious, nevertheless, delivered the exact sense of despair and inevitability that was meant to be delivered.

*****

"So as you can see, this is what would have happened," said Josh.

They were back in the small room, after disengaging from the demonstration. "I had two choices with you, to include you in all this, or to leave you out of it, which means you also have two choices. You could become a Watcher like me, or I could have the Watchers erase all this and put you back in your original timeline. I would still be your sweet Uncle Josh, and none of this would have ever existed; none of this would have ever happened."

"But...I will be dead!" she says, "That does not seem to be a real choice. Wouldn't I die in the towers like everyone else?"

"Indeed," his signature word. "That would not be a choice at all. In order to be a Watcher, you need to show them who you really are. You don't just say yes. And if you choose not to, the timeline will be adjusted, you will be out of danger and will continue living in a post 9/11 world. This way, the temptation to go back to normal life is great. Being a Watcher means you will have to live with the knowledge you could potentially have saved all these lives of friends and colleagues and you didn't."

He was watching her closely now.

"Being a Watcher means that you can, in your heart of hearts, forgive me and carry on. Like Judas forgave his tormentor. Like Nathan forgave his mystery messenger. Forgive me because of what you have seen here."

"Being a Watcher means a life of solitude and almost never being able to share who you really are with those you love, almost

114

never being able to really love, to really share, to live a normal life. Being a Watcher means that you may face a choice as horrible as I had, allowing all those thousands to perish at the World Trade Center; a choice as horrible as Yehuda had to face when he took the action that led to the crucifixion."

"Being a Watcher means that you will have to make that choice."

He paused, reliving his own memories.

"And even if it doesn't come to that, being a Watcher means that at any time, you could be asked to perform what seems to be a horrendous act. All in the name of progressing to that dimension our Six tell us about, all in the name of fighting ultimate evil, all in the name of positive evolution of mankind, of our civilization, our culture, our planet, our future."

He looked at her. She looked at him, a candid look, a good one. "You have to be sure of IceFire; IceFire has to be sure of you." "Two choices?" she asked.

"Two choices."

She got it. She understood. Faint questions were fighting her enforced tranquility. There was something she used to say…what was it?

Josh knew. Gently, he ushered her to the cot. Jenna closed her eyes. "Everything has to die down for a while, die down, a small piece of peace, a tiny slice of quiet in the mayhem."

It was found that the vibrating waves of fermions travel clockwise using 10 dimensions and the vibrating waves of bosons travel counterclockwise in 26 dimensions.

From the Kaluza-Klein, theory of the universe

Chapter 9

The pain woke her; unbelievable pain, anger, waves of nausea that she felt had left her, memories of falling bodies and burning flesh. The PAIN!

As if he felt her pain, he entered and stood there silently. She raised her tear-soaked eyes.

"But why??? Why like this, why not just bring me here, why tell me before and make me go through this hell of guilt? It is hell! Why the torture?"

With the medication gone, she felt it all, as if the time spent sedated was now burdening her already weary consciousness with an extra force of guilt and fury.

"I told you," said Josh, strangely distant and estranged. "You have to feel what it like is to be a Watcher. What it is like to have the fate of mankind in your hands. What it is like to make a decision that may haunt you in your dreams and nightmares, in your sleep and wakefulness, in your happiness and sorrow, to live with it, to endure."

He turned and left. She stared after him, eyes blinded by tears. "I hate this!" she yelled. "I hate all of this and you, I hate YOU!"

And then, her mind's remote corner was engaged with something that she had heard not long before. Something that can…yes! A thought. No, not a thought, a touch. YES! A touch, his touch on her skin. If he could do it, so could she! After all, that's what she does. Isn't it? That's what she IS.

She can see logic. She can see patterns…what was that she used to say—what was it she learned from her college professor, in that final lecture about landing a job out there in the real world? What was it?

Oh yes, never just two choices, there is always a third way, you just have to find it, to fight for it. Yes, that's it!

What was it he used to say? Yes, always look for the other way, the back door, climbing through the fire escape, showing up with fresh pastries, Knicks tickets, something for the wife, the husband, the boyfriend, the girlfriend, the daughter, the pet; figure out what moves the needle, yes! Yes!!!

The touch! The sensation! She can duplicate it! She is memory Jenna. She is code-cracking Jenna! As endless parades of office polls and NY Times puzzles can attest to.

Her fingers were probing; does she have enough of the strange liquid in her system? Will she really be able to make that journey? Is the Watchers' blood coursing through her veins enough to guide her? Could she use it against its original purpose?

Was she thinking about time? Was she thinking about traveling through it? Could she reach her destination? Was she still thinking about the New York Times crossword puzzle?

Is she still thinking about office polls? Office polls…

Office…

"Jenna, are you ready with the specs?"

Office,

Chair,

Screen, LCD,

AC humming…

Where was she?

IceFire voice? No, but no accent.

"Jenna?"

Who was talking to her? Why did her head feel like cotton balls were stuffed in her eardrums?

Reality rush! Here. She made it. She made it!

"Jenna?"

Kenneth's voice showed concern.

"Kenneth? Is that you?"

"Of course, it is me. Are you OK? All of a sudden, I lost you there."

They were sitting in the conference room; laptops and charts covered the table surface and posters of Warhol on the walls. The window glowed with September blue, and the church spire across the street was glistening in the afternoon sun of a crisp, pleasant New York City fall day, just a slight hint of leaves changing colors.

A faint echo of street sounds, coming through the half-open window, was background to the silent, familiar hum that surrounded her.

September glow…what was it that was so urgent in her head, cotton balls melting away?

Blood rushing, yes! I am here!

"Kenneth!" she grabbed his arm. Surprised, he held his calm. "What day is today, Kenneth? What day?" Jenna was tense. Erratic. He looked at her with half-a-worried smile.

"A case of stormy Monday; it must have been something really strong."

"Cut the crap, Kenneth," she snapped. "Is it Monday or not?"

"What's with you?" Polite concern, his signature communication device, felt so familiar.

"Sure, it is Monday, but…"

She cut him off, "Monday? What's the date, Kenneth? The date!" "Jenna, seriously, I thought you weren't doing this anymore." "Damn you, Kenneth, the goddamn date!"

He moved the digital clock from across the table and the red digits read 09/10/01.

As she stared at the clock, she heard the echoes of faint screams and smelled ashes and burned flesh…

Kenneth spoke.

"Jenna, what's wrong with you? Our presentation to the client is due in 20 minutes. You've gotta get it together!"

She focused.

"Forget the presentation, Kenneth, I gotta, I gotta, I gotta." "Gotta what?"

"9/11, that's it," she got up, "Sorry, Kenneth. Gotta go. You hold the fort." Before he managed to respond, she was gone and on her phone.

"Police, 1st precinct; what is your emergency?"

"A terrible disaster is going to happen!" Jenna yelled unaware of the staring bystanders around her as she walked down the hallway.

"Ma'am, has a crime been committed?" "Not yet, but by tomorrow…"

The tired voice behind the receiver sighed almost visibly.

"Ma'am, I can't help you with tomorrow. This is today. Are you calling to report a crime?"

Jenna yelled, "You've gotta listen to me. I know what's going to happen; you have to…oh, forget it," she slammed the phone down and headed for the stairs.

Even in her near hysteria state of mind, Jenna knew that the 911 algorithm (the irony didn't escape her) will push her call to the bottom of the barrel. Stephanie told her all about how the 911 system is programed to fend of 'garbage' calls. Even now, she could remember it. She will have to go there, in person, to confront, to convince.

She was sitting in the small room with strange calmness. The bare-walled room contained a folding table, a glass of water, paint chipping at the edges of the walls, visible stains on the infamous two-way mirror, ugly tiles, and harsh neon lights cruelly exposing the stains and cracks. "1984" flushed in her head. Jenna never found herself in one of these rooms, 'the box' in Law-and-Order speak, first time for everything. Huh! How understated a statement of her current state; irony-seeking mind never rests, not even now.

She was calm, after bursting into the precinct, after the officers trying to calm her down. After her yelling, "Al Qaeda," and the man in the ill-fitting suit jerked his head up and his gaze locked with hers. FBI—he knew! He knew! She had delivered the message!

And now, waiting in this room, surely they were going to alert the airports. History could be changed! He listened to her so intently, his eyes shining with empathy as she rambled about the towers. She must have succeeded in making him aware, they must have been suspecting already. FBI MUST have some idea about what's going to happen; they must, they must!

He didn't even ask her how she knew, he was taken by the truth. The door opened.

Three people entered: Dean the FBI agent, a man in uniform, and another civilian who held a briefcase and wore glasses. The last man was middle-aged, somewhat balding, and wore a detached look. The man in uniform was anything but detached, intense, eyes like canons shooting at her from a hostile foxhole. Military.

"So you are an Al-Qaeda agent," said the military man. Jenna stared at him with blank eyes.

"She is not even denying," said the civilian. Senses rushed back.

"No! No! No!" she pleaded. "Don't you get it? I am here to warn you about what they are planning! In less than a day, they are going to fly planes into…"

"And you know that, how…?" The retort was cold and hostile.

"You don't get it! I am here to warn you! I am not a terrorist. Please, you have to believe me, you have to!"

"Once again, how do you know that?"

Even in that advanced stage of near hysteria, Jenna knew that talks about IceFire, time travel and alternate timelines would not fly here.

"I can't tell you," she said. "But you have to believe me, you simply have to. You have to call the White House, evacuate the Pentagon, close down the airports…" Her voice trailed as she looked at the people standing in front of her.

Dean spoke, "Jenna, you must know what you sound like. Close airports? Evacuate the Pentagon?" He paused, letting her hear the enormity of her own words.

"Really? You really think that we are going to do that on the word of an obviously disturbed individual?" His powerful words arrested her tongue. She could only stare at him through tearful eyes.

"What we need to know is how you know the term 'Al-Qaeda'," said Dean quietly. "That is not public knowledge; how did you know that?"

Jenna jumped to her feet and screeched, "I told you. I told you! I know what is going to happen. I saw it! I was there! You have to believe me!"

Firm hands clamped down on her shoulders and as she tried to fight the restraining hold, she could see the civilian opening his case. She tried to break free. She struggled.

"No, don't drug me. You don't understand, thousands of people are going to die. The towers!"

Her voice trailed off as the needle hit home. Dean gave a slight expression of concern. There was a predatory look from the military man.

Darkness.

"So, none of this was real," he nodded.

They were back in the small white room. She didn't even have the energy to be angry anymore, to be sad, to feel guilt, to feel SOMETHING.

"I almost miss that," escaped her lips.

"Miss what?"

"The pain, anger, something. You completely blocked me with this; you left me nothing to cover myself with, to cover my mind with. Did you have to do this? Did you?" Plaintively.

"You did it to yourself, remember?" Time for a mental slap on the wrist, he thought, unwillingly performing what needed to be performed.

She recoiled.

So did he; after all, she WAS his beloved niece. Deep under the armor, he was still, and would always be her Uncle Josh, one way or another.

"I am truly sorry for this," he said.

He knew though; she was after all his niece; he knew she would not give up.

"You didn't believe me. You thought you could go back and change that which could not be changed. You thought you had a third choice where in fact, there was no third choice."

Just stating the facts, this quiet voice ripped into her more than all the screams she had buried in her memory.

Jenna felt lost; not even her pain or her anger remained to guide her. To keep her company, to give her a feeling of connection to her old self, to her old Jenna, to before all this, she felt detached. She felt her humanity, everything she knew, everything that she WAS. It all became different; maybe it was all gone; maybe this is what it was like to be a Watcher. She tried to feel that sense of loss she felt for her family, her friends, her Stephanie, wonderful lovely Stephanie, her Chris, beloved Chris…her city, her beloved city, World Trade Center spears kissing the sky… She could MAKE herself feel the longing, but …

He watched her; he knew; he must have known. After all, he went through this too. The thought comforted her. Brought her back from the depths that were threatening to overpower her. She was still Jenna, even with all of this.

Long silence.

"So, what now?" she asked. "You know I am not convinced. I know there was no other way, but I can't feel it inside me. My head agrees with you, but my heart doesn't."

Josh smiled. Jenna looked at him, perplexed, why this good, honest smile? Didn't she just tell him that all this was in vain? That she could not do what he wanted her to do? That she could not be who he wanted her to be? Didn't she just seal her fate as a failed Watcher? Like this Nathan person?

Josh started to nod slowly, his smile widening. Jenna was looking at him, puzzled.

"Oh, Jenna, I knew I could count on you. You see, this was the last test, a test of honesty, a test of courage, and you passed it. You would not accept my word; you would not accept IceFire's word; you would not even accept your own word, your own experience, honest to the end. This is what a true Watcher needs to be."

"But…"

"I know you can't feel it yet; come, we are going inside."

"I thought we already did that."

"No, we only went to the oval, to the IceFire surface, a tourist vantage."

He smiled and she smiled back; even now, even here, his smile still had this…this restorative power, a gentle reminder from a gentle time. *Ah, Uncle, sometimes the little things make all the difference.*

"And I am not to be a tourist anymore?" "Not anymore," he agreed.

"Time to get real?" she asked. "Time to get real," he echoed.

"Funny," she said with a sliver of her Jenna self. "I actually don't know if REAL the right word to use here is."

She shot a quick look at him and saw his nod of approval; a slight comic relief, always welcome.

"But hey, you are the one watching over this show, no pun intended."

He chuckled softly; this, a good time for a chuckle, before going inside, underneath the surface.

*****

Jihad is obligatory for Muslims.

Abu Bakr

Sons of Islam everywhere, the jihad is a duty—to establish the rule of Allah on earth and to liberate your countries and yourselves from America's domination and its Zionist allies, it is your battle, either victory or martyrdom.

Ahmed Yassin

"UISA"

For once, it seemed to Moe it was a good thing Marlene could no longer tend the 'bar', or whatever they were calling it these days.

The badly photocopied, clumsily put together flyer was burning a hole in his back pocket as well as in his mind all day long.

It was the crack of dawn when the last of the enforcers left, after they had nearly drained Moe's puny supply of forbidden spirits. They did not rush to their morning prayer in the neighborhood mosque.

"Don't worry, Musa," they sloppily patted him on his shoulders, as they strapped on their AK47s and handguns, adjusting their red and white caphias at a jaunty angle.

"We will take care of you. This is Ramadan, the holiest of holy times, the month when Allah gave the holy book to the believers, and another shipment is coming."

Just as the last one finally left the doorway, and as Moe was heading back to his cramped back office to tally up the night's receipts (more like night's losses as money didn't much change hands at all), he heard a quick 'Swish', went back to the door and there it was.

He picked it up absently, usually this type of communication was pure junk, a new mosque opening, a class on how to adjust better to the life of faith, the latest fashion in appropriate burqa attire, halal course for beginners and advanced, invitation to the mall square for display of public justice, that sort of thing.

He was ready to discard the unwanted intrusion when something caught his eye. Could it be?

Surely, it could not, but there it was—the almost forgotten image of a young woman's smile, eyes and teeth glittering, soft *red curls framing decisive cheekbones and upturned nose, green eyes...*

The flyer dropped from his hands.

This was unthinkable, this was dangerous, this was... He could not think straight for a few seconds. Then he felt compelled; he picked the now crumpled piece of paper and rushed to the back office.

Locked door, light, quick check of windows, privacy, good.

Next to the unreal picture, in hard-to-read type, the product of a cheap copy machine, it said:

"No, this is not a joke, this is for real. This is for you. If you can still remember the days of running freely in the park, of parties on the beach, of GOING to the beach, of shorts and bikinis, of men and women working together side by side, of cops and firefighters hanging out in a bar, of a glass of red with your steak,   a glass of white with your calamari strips... If you remember all that, then know this:

WE HAVE ALL THIS! We are hidden; we are so far from the main grid. The mullahs don't know or don't care about us. We are deep in what was known as the Blue Mountain reservation, and we would like YOU to join us. To feel again the free air, the sweet breeze, church bells if you wish, shofar blast if that's your pleasure, incense for your deity if that's what your heart desires; please remember—we put our life in your hands with this flyer, but we decided it is worth the risk...

So if you are ready to risk with us, for the chance of lost life come again, then head to the Blue Mountains from wherever you are. There, in the forgotten limbo of what was known as the heartland, on the shores of a forgotten lake, there you will find us.

Take this flyer with you. We have sent word to those in the know. Hopefully, you will find them and they will find you; we offer no promises, just a hope."

His name, Moe, was hand-written in the top right-hand corner of this...this...incriminating letter. What was he to do?

He was deep in thought. Moe used to play football millions of years ago.

His face proudly carried some scarring from those long-forgotten days. His face, not really good looking but with a compelling honesty to it, was usually bright and open. When he was deeply thinking about something, which didn't happen much, the scar on his forehead would contort a bit, as if it had a life of its own. It was an endearing sight to Marlene in those happier days when she was there to share his day with him, no more.

"Think, Moe, think!"

The first impulse was to light a match and burn this piece of heresy to ashes.

Forget about what he saw, even convince himself that it never happened. After all, life wasn't too bad in the new order. Unlike many of his neighbors, he was able to hold on, even when the ban on liquor was put into effect by the second Shariat congress... He, Moe, was a master of adapting, and the foresight of storing some choice merchandise paid off when the enforcers came.

They found his stockpile almost immediately and he died, right then and there, the sick sweat of fear in his eyes, fear of public stoning or beheading or worse—being sent to those "camps" where supposedly you were being conditioned to become one of the faithful. Many were taken; none were returned.

From his delirious state of shock, he could hear laughing in appreciation. That jolted him back to painful consciousness.

"Very good, Musa, very good indeed," Hajj, the burly enforcer commander was saying, holding a bottle of Grey Goose. "You kept the best."

A weak "what" managed to escape Moe's lips.

"Come on, Musa," said amused Hajj. "You know the best goes for the best."

And there it was.

From that moment on, he knew he could keep his boat afloat. He made a deal with the devil...no, he made a deal with Allah...

For some reason, they chose his modest two-story establishment, a sixth-generation Irish pub as their oh-so-secret place for enjoying all they were denying everyone else. After all, enforcing the Sharia was thirsty work; just be discreet, Moe, and we will allow your puny, pathetic existence to continue.

So he learned; he learned to exist. Just like he learned to serve customers without Marlene, without her smile and her wit and the knowledge that she was here next to him, just like she was during the past 20 years. Yes, the day she had to leave work

127

was the day the third Shariat congress implemented what they called "the third measure of purity". As a result, women all over town, all over the state, all over the country had to quit work, for the prophet forbade that...

And home was not good for Marlene. Dick and Jane were young then, very young and very exposed. They were becoming something very different from what he had hoped for in those years gone by, when he and Marlene—M&M as they used to be called in those days—were happy. Those sweet nothings they used to whisper in each other's ears. Going online and looking for hot vacation spots, the shy smile on her lips as she paraded her new bathing suit for him...

All that rushed back now and it was all this flyer's fault! Damn! Damn! Damn!

He really thought he had it under control, that he had forgotten the sense of helplessness in those fateful years where everything was changing, a few rallies, a few political speeches, some demonstrations, some online petitions. But nothing helped; before long, going to church became eccentric, then weird, then almost impossible.

The ban on this store, on that magazine, the threat of closing the gas station if the synagogue next door was allowed to continue...the first public mosque prayer, all bacon disappearing from store shelves, apologetic manager, "We have to bend with the times, Moe. We want deliveries to continue and we can't afford a gas ban...just a modest adjustment..."

And another one, and another one, and here we are.

"Here we are," Moe said aloud. Damn this flyer! Why now, why when he already made peace with his home-imprisoned wife, with his overlords treating him as a half-pet. Half sub-human, with his militant Muslim kids, with the colors gone from his childhood streets, why now?

So all day, all this long, drawn-out Ramadan day, he labored away, getting ready for tonight, the last night of holy Ramadan, the loudest and the longest. All day, he prepared and that whole time, the flyer was in his pocket, safely tucked between some old bills. What do I do, what do I do?

And now, on the road in his beat-up pickup, he finally decided, the hell with it!

He couldn't even recognize his kids anymore. Every meal, every outing, the simplest activity turned into agony with "blessed the prophet" this and "this is the way of the faithful" that, the hell with it! He will tell Marlene and together, they will head out to the Blue Mountains, to look for that last breath of fresh air, that last shred of happier times, of their previous life...if it still exists...

*****

Love of the world is the root of all evil.

Muhammad

Chapter 10

Jenna emerged slowly yet again, eyes and senses slowly… receding from the heightened state of awareness, not fully in control. Yet she realized where she was, no, where she WILL be, a sensation not unlike a gentle caressing as IceFire's matter disengages…

Better to just close eyes, better to just close senses, better to… "Again? You did it to me again?" She blamed her uncle. "This time, it was a bit different, wasn't it?"

Josh, cool as a cucumber beside her.

"This time, you knew. I told you what would happen. It was different." A statement, not a question.

"Yes," she says. It WAS different. This time, it wasn't voices inside her mind. This time she was LIVING the story. It was like…like…like sitting in a 3D presentation—remember Jenna? That crazy guy, years ago, this crazy guy and his new technology; 3D commercials will take the advertising world by storm, he said… Only it was a lot more than 3D, sights and smells, feelings and sounds. Not their voices inside her head, but SHE inside their heads, INSIDE their heads; this was no 3D, this was…this was…

"IceFire's multi-dimension," said Josh. "What did I tell you?"

"So THAT'S where you go to see those futures. Inside Ice Fire!" Understanding at last.

"This is where you go to get these memories!" "That and more. Look around you, Jenna."

She complied, and little by little, she realized that reality was different. IceFire was flickering in a way that she couldn't see before. Her mind jumped back to the warped endless line of mirrors at the gym, Jenna reflected times infinity…

Shades of meaning present themselves to her, shades…

Vertigo invaded, overpowering her senses. It took effort to not let it control her.

"You can turn it off at will," Josh's steadying hand on her elbow as she almost collapsed. "How?"

"Think it," he said and she did.

And it stopped. "What the…"

"This is a 36 vision, Jenna; you have been inside IceFire, even briefly and without consciousness. You carry a 36 vision now."

"A 36 vision?"

"Yes, you now have veils. You now can see veils and soon, you will be able to use veils."

"Not another fortune cookie," she tried to smile but failed. Her tired mind knew that this was a pivotal moment, sensation first, understanding second. This was a very difficult prospect for ever-logical Jenna. Her ancestors did say in their forty-year desert journey, "We shall do and then, we shall understand." This wasn't her; Jenna operated with her quick and rational mind. So many things have changed; this will change too.

What she did know, in her bones, was that this was serious. This…transformation? This…metamorphosis? This…mutation?

This was a serious time. This was a serious business. "And these…veils are what I am supposed to use for…"

IceFire's voice inside her head made its presence known; funny, she now almost welcomed it. IceFire was on its way to becoming almost an extension to her consciousness; an ever-present entity; dormant yet ready to spring to action whenever needed, a potent tool on her potent tool belt. IceFire was ready to impart knowledge, his knowledge and predecessor's knowledge, to impart experience, his experience, predecessor's experience, hers was the entire Watchers' experience to learn from.

Scary.

"Yes, Jenna, you started the process of becoming a Watcher. Go back to your previous thoughts; go back to your doubts; what do you feel now?"

She does and…

And…

Eyes darting to him, he nods his head from left to right. Nope, she is 100% Jenna, no mental Advil, no artificial tranquility coursing through her veins and yet…

"Pain is gone," she whispered, and it was true. The pain and anger WERE gone, so was the loneliness. Only a vast, immense sadness remained; it had an address, this sadness... It had a face, a form, a feel, a sensation of an old pickup truck bumping its way on a dirt road, a feeling of...

She remembered now. She remembered the crumpled flyer in the back pocket. She remembered the sweet sweat of excitement and fear. She remembered it all; she remembered it as if it were her anticipation, her excitement, and her fear.

"Did he make it?" she asked IceFire inside her head. "Did he make it with his wife to the Blue Mountains?"

"Does it matter? It never really happened. Remember, Little One?"

"To me, it does," she insisted. Before she could complete the thought, she knew he didn't. She knew the flyer was a ruse planted by his kids. She knew the Shariat police picked him up there in that reality/non-reality simulation. Then she knew. Then she believed. Then she was. She felt the pieces of her mind, of her soul, of her Jenna self and of her Watcher self. She felt how snowflakes were descending slowly and settling at exact coordinates on the landscape of her mind. She remembered how, not long ago, she was one of these snowflakes. What she was to IceFire. What she was becoming to IceFire. She felt quiet elation mixed with the sweetest sadness she could ever feel.

A tear escaped her eye.

She thought she had no more tears left after the oceans of tears spilled for her friends and colleagues who were burned and suffocated, who jumped from death by flames to death by pavement. She shed tears for Stephanie whom she can never enjoy in the same way again, for Chris, for her friends and parents... She thought there WERE no more tears to shed.

But here there was one more, not for her real past, but for her unreal side-future. For Moe and Marlene, M&M, heading west in their pickup. Moe and Marlene. Smiling and talking about sharing a cold beer by a warm fire with friends. Talking about dancing and music, about...

She welcomed that tear. It was as if it connected her human self and her 36 self into her Jenna self.

Jenna was silent for a long time.

Then she started to pick up the pieces. The discarded pieces of patterns, of meanings of hidden significance, kicked into turbo gear, into Jenna mode.

"Shades," she whispered. "Something about shades." Josh nodded in disbelief.

"So quick," he whispered.

She opened her eyes and looked at him.

"It was Stephanie, right?" she said. " She was wearing shades to hide her eyes, right? That…EVIL IceFire was talking about doing something to her."

Josh paid her the immense compliment of silent intense listening.

"And you knew. You came and took me. Now I remember. Taking the stairs, the SUV that made you take that alley, was it really there?"

And her mind exploded yet again.

"Wait, that was another dimension, right? Another veil that you took me to! I know. Those street signs; they were strange. Your new car… Your living room, another reality, right? Once removed?"

Josh clapped his hands.

"Amazing, one moment you breathe fire at me, and the next you're a 36 through and through." He smiled a warm smile and Jenna felt that there was a reservoir of force that could serve to fill the emptiness that presented itself to her. "Hey, there is some humanity in being a 36 after all."

"So, this is how it works?" she asked. "What else do I need to know?"

"Transition almost complete," he thought.

"May I?" He reached to the back of her neck. He was about to perform the most unpleasant task in a long line of such tasks; inevitable though, it had to be done.

When they disengaged, her eyes were wide open, overwhelmed, yet guarded. Josh was as pleased as he could have been. Jenna had just been through the very unpleasant experience of meeting the power of the Circle. She'd been from fire to mountain to temple to tunnel; human sacrifice, Gonars, all of them, experienced sheer triumphant evil. It was an evil, which feasted on fear, greed, pain, and horror. It fed on flesh and blood and bones and endless screams of terror.

She collected herself.

"Fortunately," said Josh. "Fortunately, every venture like the ones you just experienced requires human life and nowadays, this is a more and more complicated task. That's why I can say 'fortunately' while relating to the unbelievable suffering of these poor souls. You see, Jenna, I remember times when human life was *a lot* more expendable."

She accepted that statement.

"But why the shades?" she asked.

"You see," he said, "In its heart, the Circle is a destructive power; a chaotic power. This is why the eyes of its human agents rotate uncontrollably. It is the only way they can physically form a symbiotic relationship with the Circle without losing their hold on reality. After all, they are people. Normally, they would not be able to communicate with The Circle. This is the mistake the Watchers made in ancient times that resulted in so many deaths."

"But the rotation does make it easier for them. And it does make it easier for the 36 to spot potential dangers. It also explains why so many people wear shades at night and indoors." He smiled. "You see, fortunately very few in the world truly serve the Circle, though a lot believe that they do."

She mirrored his smile with a pale version of her own. He hadn't told her everything though, not yet.

"The Circle has dominion over this world," he continued.

"Dominion over the number one world or number one veil, if you will. In part, because it knows no boundaries, and in part, because it made a bond with matter that is strong beyond the power of the Watchers. The Circle is not interested in reuniting with the original dimension, the place which they all came from, both the Circle and the Watchers."

"All the Circle wants is to feed on matter; on flesh and blood. The Watchers' advantages are their ability to foresee events and to temporarily enter other timelines. They have the power to manipulate all dimensions of time and matter, but they do so very carefully so as to not hamper their chances of achieving their ultimate goal. Some of these skills we learn from them. But the Circle can copy us, at least to an extent. If we practice our foresight, the Circle may be able to see what we see."

She nodded.

"When we enter another veil of this world, the Circle may be able to follow us. Only here, in IceFire sanctuary, we are completely safe, well, almost."

Another wave of understanding washed over her.

"What I felt just before I woke up and as I was waking up…"

Josh was ready, he was glad that THAT particular realization came now, at the right time, his niece being already armed with a 36 vision.

"Yes, you woke up with the beginning of a Watcher activity in you. The Circle is very sensitive to this; think about all the billions of minds on earth and only 36 display certain… patterns."

"So, I was marked?"

"You were."

"Well, thank you for telling me now, dear Uncle." Her smile defied her words.

They were now communicating on a different plane, comrades, brothers-in-arms; still a little piece of the past balance remained. For both, it was very important to hold on to it, to hold on to each other. They knew, this didn't need to be communicated.

"To what end?" what she was asking Josh was academic.

"Any number of things, darling Niece, incinerate your brain then and there, sending Stephanie to deliver you to the Circle as a hostage; a ceremonial victim…"

He stopped, watching the impact. She was as sardonic as he, good. "There is more."

"Yes," he agreed. "The Circle can prevent the making of a 36."

"Prevent?"

"It, of course, could have tried to kill you. But remember, the Circle feasts on suffering, and what is better than to watch its archenemy suffer. The suffering of a failed Watcher is a prime target for the Circle, lasting millennia, among its most desirable prizes."

"Nathan Straus," said Jenna. "I was wondering why his voice sounded so different, so very sad."

"He ended up not doing what needed to be done," replied Josh. "He was supposed to cause an outbreak of a disease during World War I that would have…"

"Killed Hitler," whispered Jenna, the enormity of that revelation hitting home. A different realization of how her life, herself, her EXISTENCE, was forever changed. Erased and re-written may have been more appropriate.

Still. Hitler, think about that; World War II was Hitler's war; no Hitler, no war. Poor Nathan, spending eternity knowing what he could have prevented. "I hope that when my time comes, I will have the power to do what needs to be done," she was thinking.

"It was one of our greatest setbacks," agreed Josh, "But Nathan is one of the good ones."

He paused, watching the perplexed look on her face. Perhaps it was too early to disclose what he was about to disclose, a judgment call.

"No, he wasn't," Josh repeated. "Time and again, a failed Watcher could turn into a real villain, delivering and inflicting the Circle's evil on the world, Nathan resisted that temptation."

There were questions, but she remained silent, feeling that now was not the time to dig deeper into this particular subject. Good, his gamble proved successful.

Her eyes changed focus again.

"You said something else before," she said. "You said…almost top prize, what else is there; what else could the Circle want?"

"You didn't miss that one, did you?" smiled her uncle, a rhetorical statement.

Josh knew that Jenna rarely missed anything, and now with her new focus and power, even less.

She was eyeing him, open yet guarded. Josh noticed a new expression, her chin etched with resolve, humorous eyes shining with new strength. What a marvelous thing she was; how he longed for this to happen; how afraid he was of this happening.

And now, he could breathe a sigh of relief.

"The most dangerous time for us is between when a 36 starts to be aware and when he or she becomes a 36; you see, this is the time when the Circle actually has a chance to invade and a chance to reach IceFire. There is no telling what would happen if an event like that took place, and you know your uncle, the last thing I want to be is overly dramatic."

It took time to digest. She was realizing the kind of danger she escaped and the kind of dangers she would face. She had more questions about all this, but she felt that now wasn't the time. Now was the time to listen, to learn, to be. Questions can be asked later.

They were silent for a moment, deriving strength and comfort from each other. "You see," he said, "we are fighting a hard fight, a dangerous one, and we suffer casualties. But we are not without power. We can see better, and we can turn to the veils for some peace, for an avenue of escape, and we have guidance from the Six."

"And you are recruiting me as a replacement for you," she said softly.

He expected that.

"Will you…where will you go?" Plaintive. In some corner of her mind, she was still just his niece.

"No need to worry about that just yet," he said. "We, the 36 have a way with time. You will return to veil 1. Stephanie will have a bit of a headache, and you will finish dinner. Just remember to watch for shades. Well, there is more to it than that, but all in good time."

They exchanged another smile.

No words needed to be said then; just the flow of time, of vision, of her new perspective, of a start.

For the first time since the forgotten silly night talk with Stephanie, back on September 10, Jenna felt like the answers were more numerous than the questions. She felt the calm was larger than the storm. She welcomed the change in herself and could now make peace with those drastic events that etched their mark deep inside her thoughts and feelings. The global and the personal; she was welcoming this new stability, this new strength.

IceFire was silent with her, and yet there was background sound, very faint. Maybe it was the sound of time passing. Never had she known such calmness or such tranquility. She could feel herself wanting to stay here forever, yet she knew that there was joy to be had. There was work to be done. She passed a test and entered a new existence. There could very well be a task in her future. All these other questions would have to be answered later.

After all, she was now a 'Lamed Vav'.

A Talmudic legend from ancient Israel came to life. Jenna, with her red curls, slanted green eyes, and upturned nose, hardly the picture of scholarly, rabbinical wisdom. But there she was, a new recruit, engines humming softly. Treading on the edge of... becoming ready for...

Finally, Josh spoke.

"Now you are ready."

"Ready for what?"

"Ready to start preparing for your first assignment."

"Really?" she said. "What's the rush? We just got here." Smiling innocently at her beloved uncle. "Can't we stay a little while longer?"

He smiled back, taking note of the undercurrent of humor and sass, good! The more human you are, the better Watcher you become.

"Assignments take time to prepare," he said.

"Ah," said Jenna, "so, you and your shiny friends DO have something specific in mind."

His silence was an acknowledgment.

"And how long do I have before this task?" she asked. "Just curious..."

"About a decade."

"Oh really, that long huh? And is it going to be another unpleasant fall surprise like the one that brought me here?"

Josh beamed, enjoying this new level of candid and frank talk. She sounded like she was a Watcher for years, not hours.

"Not exactly," he said. "You may want to think about it in terms of spring."

"Spring?"

"Spring."

"Okie dokie," she said. "Where do we start?"

"We start with a history lesson."

Jenna smiled softly. History was always her favorite subject.

CPSIA information can be obtained
at www.ICGtesting.com
Printed in the USA
BVHW031647061022
648848BV00022B/346

9 781641 829472